中英双语版

长安狂醉

惊艳千年的李白诗集

许渊冲 译
刘小川 注、评

SELECTED
POEMS
OF
LIBAI

北京联合出版公司

图书在版编目（CIP）数据

长安狂醉：惊艳千年的李白诗集 / 许渊冲译；刘小川注、评. -- 北京：北京联合出版公司，2025.9.

ISBN 978-7-5596-8524-7

Ⅰ. I207.227.42

中国国家版本馆CIP数据核字第2025M0266S号

长安狂醉：惊艳千年的李白诗集

译　　者：许渊冲
注　　者：刘小川
评　　者：刘小川
出 品 人：赵红仕
责任编辑：刘　恒
封面设计：吴黛君

北京联合出版公司出版
（北京市西城区德外大街83号楼9层 100088）
北京新华先锋出版科技有限公司发行
三河市兴博印务有限公司印刷　新华书店经销
字数148千字　787毫米×1092毫米　1/32　8印张
2025年9月第1版　2025年9月第1次印刷
ISBN 978-7-5596-8524-7
定价：49.00元

版权所有，侵权必究
未经书面许可，不得以任何方式转载、复制、翻印本书部分或全部内容。
本书若有质量问题，请与本社图书销售中心联系调换。电话：（010）88876681-8026

目录

辑一 树深时见鹿

访戴天山道士不遇	002
登锦城散花楼	004
峨眉山月歌	006
巴女词	008
荆州歌	010
渡荆门送别	012
望庐山瀑布水（二首其二）	014
望庐山五老峰	016
望天门山	018
杨叛儿	020
长干行（二首其一）	022
长干行（二首其二）	026
金陵酒肆留别	030
夜下征虏亭	032
上李邕	034

1

静夜思	036
黄鹤楼送孟浩然之广陵	038
长相思（二首其一）	040
长相思（二首其二）	042
登新平楼	044

辑二　长风破浪会有时

蜀道难	048
行路难（三首其一）	054
行路难（三首其二）	056
行路难（三首其三）	060
送友人入蜀	064
春夜洛城闻笛	066
塞下曲（六首其一）	068
关山月	070
乌夜啼	072
春思	074
三五七言	076
怨情	078
玉阶怨	080

长门怨（二首其一）	082
长门怨（二首其二）	084
子夜吴歌（春歌）	086
子夜吴歌（夏歌）	088
子夜吴歌（秋歌）	090
子夜吴歌（冬歌）	092

辑三　与尔同销万古愁

将进酒	096
赠孟浩然	100
夜泊牛渚怀古	102
客中行	104
陌上赠美人	106
登太白峰	108
登广武古战场怀古	110
南陵别儿童入京	114
清平调词（三首其一）	116
清平调词（三首其二）	118
清平调词（三首其三）	120
忆东山（二首其一）	122

乌栖曲	124
下终南山过斛斯山人宿置酒	126
月下独酌（四首其一）	128
把酒问月	130
白云歌送刘十六归山	134

辑四　我寄愁心与明月

秋日鲁郡尧祠亭上宴别杜补阙范侍御	138
鲁郡东石门送杜二甫	140
沙丘城下寄杜甫	142
戏赠杜甫	144
梦游天姥吟留别	146
登金陵凤凰台	152
劳劳亭	154
丁都护歌	156
苏台览古	158
越中览古	160
越女词（五首其一）	162
越女词（五首其三）	164
越女词（五首其五）	166

渌水曲	168
闻王昌龄左迁龙标遥有此寄	170
战城南	172

辑五　举杯消愁愁更愁

听蜀僧濬弹琴	178
寄东鲁二稚子	180
秦王扫六合	184
登高丘而望远海	188
北风行	192
横江词（六首其一）	196
山中问答	198
自遣	200
独坐敬亭山	202
宣州谢朓楼饯别校书叔云	204
秋登宣城谢朓北楼	206
送友人	208
秋浦歌（十七首其十四）	210
秋浦歌（十七首其十五）	212
赠汪伦	214

哭晁卿衡	216
永王东巡歌（十一首其二）	218
与史郎中钦听黄鹤楼上吹笛	220

辑六　轻舟已过万重山

早发白帝城	224
与夏十二登岳阳楼	226
陪族叔刑部侍郎晔及中书 　贾舍人至游洞庭（五首其二）	228
江上吟	230
夜宿山寺	232
庐山谣寄卢侍御虚舟	234
豫章行	238
哭宣城善酿纪叟	242
宣城见杜鹃花	244
临终歌	246

辑一

树深时见鹿

访戴天山①道士不遇②

犬吠③水声中,
桃花带露浓④。
树深⑤时见鹿,
溪午不闻钟。
野竹分青霭⑥,
飞泉挂碧峰。
无人知所去,
愁倚⑦两三松。

①戴天山:位于今四川省江油市,李白青年时期曾在此山中的大明寺读书。
②不遇:没有遇到。
③吠:狗叫。
④带露浓:挂满了露珠。
⑤树深:树丛深处。
⑥青霭:青色的云气。
⑦倚:靠。

这首诗通篇着意于写景,生动形象地再现了道士世外桃源的优美生活境界。诗人远道而来,总想见到道士。末句将等待道士归来的神情刻画得极为传神。此诗虽有访友不遇的惆怅,但更多更主要的是通过对优美山川的赞美,抒发一种悠闲恬淡的情致,表达对超凡脱俗品格的仰慕和追求。

Calling on a Taoist Recluse in Daitian Mountain without Meeting Him

Dogs' barks are muffled by the rippling brook,
Peach blossoms tinged by dew much redder look.
In the thick woods a deer is seen at times;
Along the stream I hear no noonday chimes.
In the blue haze which wild bamboos divide,
Tumbling cascades hang on green mountainside.
Where has the Taoist gone? No one can tell me.
Saddened, I lean on this or that pine tree.

登锦城散花楼

日照锦城①头,
朝光散花楼。
金窗②夹绣户③,
珠箔④悬银钩⑤。
飞梯绿云中,
极目散我忧。
暮雨向三峡,
春江绕双流⑥。
今来一登望,
如上九天游。

①锦城:指锦官城,故址位于今四川省成都市南。
②金窗:华美的窗子。
③绣户:雕饰精美的门户。
④珠箔:珠帘。由珍珠穿制而成或饰有珍珠的帘子。
⑤银钩:玉制之钩。
⑥双流:县名,属成都府,今为双流区。

  旭日初升,霞光映照,散花楼更显金碧辉煌、富丽堂皇。高梯入云,楼接霄汉,气象雄伟。诗人极目云天,心旷神怡,因而流连忘返。作诗时,又再一次抒发登楼的愉悦之情。整首诗意境飘逸,开合自然。

On the Flowery Tower in the Town of Silk

The sun shines on the Town of Silk, the Tower
Is steeped in morning glow as strewn with flowers.
By golden windows and embroidered doors,
The pearly curtains hang on silver hooks.
Into green clouds a flight of stairways soars;
The gloom's dispelled at such sunny outlooks.
The evening rain towards Three Canyons flies;
Around the town wind rivers crystal-clear.
Today I come to feast on this my eyes
As if I visited Celestial Sphere.

峨眉山[1]月歌

峨眉山月半轮秋[2],
影入平羌[3]江水流。
夜发[4]清溪向三峡,
思君不见下渝州[5]。

[1]峨眉山:位于今四川省乐山市。
[2]半轮秋:半圆的秋月。
[3]平羌:江名,即今青衣江,位于峨眉山东北。
[4]发:出发。
[5]渝州:今重庆一带。

这是李白初离蜀地赴长江中下游的舟行途中所作,写诗人在舟中所见的夜景。全诗连用五个地名,精巧地点出行程,通过山月和江水展现了一幅千里蜀江行旅图,既有"仗剑去国,辞亲远游"的豪迈,也有依恋家乡山水的情怀。该诗意境清朗秀美,语言流转自然,恰似"清水出芙蓉,天然去雕饰",充分展示了青年李白的艺术天赋。

The Moon over the Eyebrow Mountains

The crescent moon looks like old Autumn's golden brow,
Its deep reflection flows with limpid water blue.
I'll leave the town on Clear Stream for Three Canyons now.
O Moon, how I miss you when you are out of view!

巴女^①词

巴水^②急如箭,
巴船去若飞。
十月三千里,
郎行几岁归?

①巴:今四川省东部和重庆市一带,古时为巴国。巴女,即巴地的女子。
②巴水:水名,在今湖北省境内。

  谁见巴水急如箭?谁睹巴船去若飞?水之急是分别之痛,船若飞乃思妇之心。夫始别,思归已切,正是郎行千里巴女痴心!读来似民歌般明快自然而不饰雕琢。时空拉长的思念动人而惆怅啊,却被而今发达的通信变短,可叹!

Song of a Woman of Ba

The River fast like arrow flows;
Your boat as if on wings swift goes.
Ten months, a thousand miles away.
When will you come back? On what day?

荆州歌[1]

白帝城[2]边足风波,
瞿塘[3]五月谁敢过?
荆州麦熟茧成蛾,
缲丝[4]忆君头绪多。
拨谷飞鸣奈妾何?[5]

[1]荆州歌:古题乐府《杂曲歌辞》。
[2]白帝城:古城名。位于今重庆市奉节县东白帝山上。
[3]瞿(qú)塘:瞿塘峡,长江三峡之一。
[4]缲(sāo)丝:制丝时把丝从蚕茧中抽出来,合并成丝。
[5]拨谷飞鸣奈妾何:拨谷鸟开始鸣叫,春天将尽,不见夫回,叫人无可奈何。

仲夏五月,阳光灿烂,江陵城外,农家院内,一位少妇,埋头缲丝。蚕茧白白,麦香淡淡,布谷声声。少妇放慢了手的动作,心情渐渐变得十分沉重。她想起了出门在外、行将归来的丈夫。这首诗便是抓住少妇在这种情境下的心理变幻来写的。五月瞿塘峡水流湍急,水中礁石林立,行船极其危险,白帝城江面也满是狂风掀起的惊涛骇浪。丈夫就要经此归来,

The Silk Spinner

The White King Town's seen many shipwrecks on the sands.
Who dare to sail through Three Canyons in the fifth moon?
The wheat is ripe; the silkworm has made its cocoon.
My thoughts of you are endless as the silken strands.
The cuckoos sing: "Go Home!"
When will you come to homeland?

少妇心中充满了对丈夫的无限担忧。忧虑、相思、烦恼似茧丝缠结心头,这时传来了布谷鸟的叫声,如唤"行不得也哥哥"。这既是少妇对驾舟欲行的丈夫的劝阻,也是少妇内心的自责,只能徒然叹道:"奈妾何?"整首诗写农妇辛勤劳作之时思念远方丈夫的愁苦情境,笔触细腻,生动传神。

渡荆门[1]送别

渡远[2]荆门外,
来从楚国[3]游。
山随平野尽,
江入大荒[4]流。
月下飞天镜[5],
云生结海楼[6]。
仍怜[7]故乡水,
万里送行舟。

[1] 荆门：山名，位于今湖北省宜都市西北长江南岸。
[2] 远：远自。
[3] 楚国：楚地，指湖北一带。
[4] 大荒：广阔无边的田野。
[5] 月下飞天镜：明月倒映江水中，如同从天上飞下的镜子。
[6] 海楼：海市蜃楼，此处指江上云霞的美景。
[7] 怜：爱。

诗人来自蜀地，远在"荆门外"，而"楚国"是目的地，出了荆门山便意味着离蜀入楚。诗人常在蜀地，一朝离别，自然感慨万千。此诗虽意在描绘山水，然送别之意犹在。诗题中的"送别"应是告别故乡而不是送别朋友。诗人顺着长江远渡荆门，江水流过的蜀地也就是曾经养育过他的故乡。初次离别，他怎能不无限留恋，依依难舍呢？诗人不说自己思念故乡，而说故乡之水恋恋不舍地一路送我远行，如此用笔，越发显出自己思乡情深。

Farewell Beyond the Thorn-Gate Gorge

Leaving Mount Thorn-Gate far away
My boat pursues its eastward way.
Where mountains end begins the plain;
The river rolls to boundless main.
The moon, celestial mirror, flies;
The clouds like miraged towers rise.
The water that from homeland flows
Will follow me where my boat goes.

望庐山瀑布水（二首其二）

日照香炉①生紫烟,
遥看瀑布挂前川。
飞流直下三千尺②,
疑是银河③落九天④。

①香炉：指香炉峰，位于庐山北部。
②三千尺：形容山高，夸张说法。
③银河：指银河系构成的带状星群。
④九天：天的最高处，形容其高。

这首诗形象地描绘了庐山瀑布雄奇壮丽的景色，反映了诗人对祖国大好河山的无限热爱。首句一个"生"字，将瀑布飞泻，水汽蒸腾而上，在丽日照耀下，仿佛有座顶天立地的香炉冉冉升起了团团紫烟的景象写活了。次句一个"挂"字化动为静，惟妙惟肖地写出了瀑布像一条巨大的白练挂到了悬崖上。第三句的"飞"和"直下"生动地描绘了瀑布喷涌而出，水流势不可挡之状。末句比喻奇特，活画出了高空突兀、巨流倾泻的磅礴气势，使整个形象变得更为丰富多彩，雄奇瑰丽。不愧为庐山绝唱。

The Waterfall in Mount Lu Viewed from Afar (II)

The sunlit Censer Peak exhales incense-like cloud,
The cataract hangs like upended stream sounding loud.
Its torrent dashes down three thousand feet from high
As if the Silver River fell from azure sky.

望①庐山五老峰②

庐山东南五老峰，
青天削出金芙蓉③。
九江秀色可揽结④，
吾将此地巢云松⑤。

①望：一作"登"。
②五老峰：庐山东南部的五座山峰，形状如席地而坐的五位老翁，因此得名。
③金芙蓉：莲花的美称。
④揽结：采集。
⑤巢云松：隐居于此。

  仰望五老峰，似青天削出的金莲；俯视山下，九江秀色可揽入怀。李太白呢，天地巨幅之间一勃勃的生命，将结庐于此与云松相视。一"削"一"揽"于平淡中见豪气。一传此诗写于李白首次游庐山之时，一传写于其避安史之乱隐居庐山之时。与云松坐视真能心静似水？未必！故幸有时也是不幸。

The Five Greybeard-like Peaks
of Mount Lu Viewed from Afar

Southeast of Mountain Lu, Five Peaks of Greybeard stand

As golden lotus carved by Heaven's azure hand.

If I could drink in beauty of the Rivers Nine,

Here I would build my nest amid the cloud and pine.

望天门山①

天门中断②楚江开③,
碧水东流至此回④。
两岸青山⑤相对出⑥,
孤帆一片日边来。

①天门山：位于今安徽省马鞍山市当涂县西南长江两岸。两山隔江对峙，形同门户，故称"天门"。
②中断：指两山之间被江水隔开。
③开：断开。
④至此回：意为东流的江水在此转向北流。回，改变方向。
⑤两岸青山：指博望山和梁山。
⑥出：出现。

  李白一生遍游名山大川，留下了许多不朽杰作。此诗描写诗人舟行江中溯流而上，远望天门山的情景。只见浩荡东流的楚江冲破天门山，经两山间的狭窄通道时，激起回旋，形成波涛汹涌的奇观。第一句借山势写水的汹涌，第二句借水势衬托山的奇险。第三句表现了在舟行过程中望天门山时天门山特有的姿态，而且蕴含了舟中人的喜悦之情。第四句饱含激情，描绘了孤帆乘风破浪，越来越靠近天门山的情景，以及诗人欣然目睹名山胜景、目接神驰的情状。此诗在描绘天门山雄伟景色的同时，突出了诗人壮怀逸兴的自我形象。

Mount Heaven's Gate Viewed from Afar

Breaking Mount Heaven's Gate, the great River rolls through,

Its east-flowing green billows, hurled back here, turn north.

From the two river banks thrust out the mountains blue,

Leaving the sun behind, a lonely sail comes forth.

杨叛儿①

君歌杨叛儿,
妾劝新丰酒。
何许最关人②?
乌啼白门③柳。
乌啼隐杨花,
君醉留妾家。
博山炉④中沉香⑤火,
双烟一气凌紫霞。

①杨叛儿:本是南北朝时期歌谣,后成为乐府诗题。
②关人:牵动人心。
③白门:刘宋都城建康(今南京)城门。南朝民间情歌常常提到白门,后代指男女幽会之地。
④博山炉:一种炉盖呈重叠山形的熏炉。
⑤沉香:一种名贵的香木,放在水中即沉下去,故又名沉水香。

  君唱歌,妾劝酒,黄昏时分在金陵西门旁的大柳树下聆听乌鸦啼鸣;乌鸦归巢后渐渐停止啼鸣,在柳叶杨花之间甜蜜地憩息了,而"君"也沉醉于"妾"家了。男子的醉留,正如沉香投入炉中,爱情的火焰立刻燃烧起来,像香火化成烟,在空中追逐缠绕,渐渐地融为一体,直入云霄。这首诗中一男一女由唱歌劝酒到醉留,在封建社会是带有解放色彩的,这显然与唐代经济繁荣、社会风气比较开放有关。

A Love Song

You sing a lover's lore;
I urge you to drink more.
What touches you and me?
Crow's nest in willow tree.
Crows hide mid poplar flowers;
Drunk, you stay in my bowers.
Behold the censer and the sandalwood in fire!
Two wreaths of smoke combine and rise higher and higher.

长干行①（二首其一）

妾发初覆额，
折花门前剧。
郎骑竹马来，
绕床②弄青梅。
同居长干里③，
两小无嫌猜。
十四为君妇，
羞颜未尝开。
低头向暗壁，
千唤不一回。
十五始展眉，
愿同尘与灰。

①长干行：乐府《杂曲歌辞》调名。
②床：井栏。
③长干里：位于今江苏省南京市，当年系船民聚居之地。

这是一首写青梅竹马的爱情和离别的诗。诗以商妇的自白，用缠绵婉转的笔调，抒写了她对远出经商的丈夫真挚的爱和深深的思念。诗以时间为序，从两小无猜写到婚后，再由丈夫远行经商写到自己的忧愁和思念，笔触细腻，感情深沉，颇为动人。

Ballads of a Merchant's Wife (I)

My forehead covered by my hair cut straight,
I played with flowers plucked before the gate.
On a hobbyhorse you came upon the scene,
Around the well we played with mumes still green.
We lived close neighbors on riverside lane.
Carefree and innocent, we children twain.
I was fourteen when I became your bride;
I'd often turn my bashful face aside.
Hanging my head, I'd look towards the wall;
A thousand times I'd not answer your call.
I was fifteen when I composed my brows,
To mix my dust with yours were my dear vows.

常存抱柱信④,
岂上望夫台!
十六君远行,
瞿塘滟滪堆⑤。
五月不可触,
猿声天上哀。
门前迟行迹,
一一生绿苔。
苔深不能扫,
落叶秋风早。
八月蝴蝶黄,
双飞西园草。
感此伤妾心,
坐愁红颜老。
早晚下三巴⑥,
预将书报家。
相迎不道远,
直至长风沙。

④抱柱信:出自《庄子·盗跖篇》。尾生与一女子相约桥下,女子未至而涨水,尾生守信不肯离去,抱住桥柱不松手,最后被淹死。后以"抱柱之信"比喻坚守信约。

⑤滟(yàn)滪(yù)堆:位于瞿塘峡峡口的一块大礁石,古代又称犹豫石。每年五月涨水没礁,船只易触礁翻沉。

⑥三巴:古地名。相当于今四川嘉陵江和綦江流域以东的大部分地区,后多泛指四川。

Rather than break faith, you declared you'd die.
Who knew I'd live alone in a tower high?
I was sixteen when you went far away,
Passing Three Canyons studded with rocks grey,
Where ships were wrecked when spring flood ran high,
Where gibbons' wails seemed coming from the sky.
Green moss now overgrows before our door;
Your footprints, hidden, can be seen no more.
Moss can't be swept away: so thick it grows,
And leaves fall early when the west wind blows.
The yellow butterflies in autumn pass
Two by two o'er our western garden grass.
This sight would break my heart, and I'm afraid,
Sitting alone, my rosy cheeks would fade.
Sooner or later, you'll leave the western land.
Do not forget to let me know beforehand.
I'll walk to meet you and not call it far
To go to Long Wind Sands or where you are.

长干行（二首其二）

忆妾①深闺里，
烟尘不曾识。
嫁与长干人，
沙头②候风色③。
五月南风兴，
思君下④巴陵⑤。
八月西风起，
想君发⑥扬子。
去来悲如何，
见少离别多。

① 妾：一作"昔"。
② 沙头：沙岸上。
③ 风色：风向。
④ 下：一作"在"。
⑤ 巴陵：今湖南省岳阳市。
⑥ 发：出发。

  细腻的笔触展现出一位长干女子的深情与坚韧。诗中女子忆及往昔深闺生活的单纯，对比如今嫁为人妇后，独立沙头，眺望远方，静静地等待着风变化的日子，形象地刻画出生活的转变。随着季节流转，五月南风兴，八月西风起；她的思念也如那风，紧紧追随着远行的丈夫。诗中既有生活的烟火气，又有绵绵的情思。语言质朴自然，将女子对丈夫的牵挂与眷恋表现得真挚动人，让我们感受到古代女子在爱情中的坚守与柔情。

Ballads of a Merchant's Wife (II)

Brought up while young in inner room,

I knew nor wind nor dust that rose.

Since you became my dear bridegroom,

I've learned on Sands from where wind blows.

In the fifth moon south wind is high,

I know you're sailing the river down;

In the eighth moon west wind comes nigh,

I think you'll leave the river town.

I'm grieved to see you come and go:

We sever longer than we meet.

湘潭⑦几日到?
妾梦越风波!
昨夜狂风度,
吹折江头树。
淼淼⑧暗无边,
行人在何处?
好乘浮云骢⑨,
佳期兰渚⑩东。
鸳鸯绿蒲上,
翡翠⑪锦屏中。
自怜十五余,
颜色桃花红。
那作商人妇,
愁水复愁风!

⑦湘潭:泛指湖南一带。
⑧淼淼:形容水势浩大。
⑨浮云骢(cōng):骏马。
⑩兰渚:生长有兰草的小洲。
⑪翡翠:水鸟名。

When will you come home? Let me know

To cross the waves my dream is fleet.

Last night a violent wind blew,

Breaking the trees by riverside.

So dark the boundless waters grew!

Where could your roving ship abide?

I'd ride upon a cloud-like steed

To meet you east of River Green

Like two love birds amid the reed

Or kingfishers on silken screen.

I pity my fifteen old years,

Like blooming peach my face is warm.

But I'm a merchant's wife in tears,

Who worries over wind and storm.

金陵①酒肆②留别

风吹柳花满店香，
吴姬③压酒④劝客尝。
金陵子弟来相送，
欲行不行各尽觞⑤。
请君试问东流水，
别意与之谁短长？

①金陵：南京。
②酒肆：酒店。
③吴姬：吴地的女子，此处指卖酒女。
④压酒：古代酒酿成时，压酒槽取酒。
⑤尽觞：干杯。

　　佳句生江上，吴姬压酒香，酒香花香春草香，朋友相送心意香。首句集视觉、嗅觉、听觉于一体，一幅柳絮飘飘、酒香郁郁、春意浓浓之景不费半分力气而出；"欲行不行各尽觞"显少年心性，饱满酣畅别而不伤；"试问东流水"构思巧妙含蓄悠然，青春的风流潇洒之态与江共长。

Parting at a Tavern in Jinling

The tavern's sweetened when wind blows in willow-down;

A Southern maiden bids the guests to taste the wine.

My dear young friends have come to see me leave the town;

They drink their cups and I, still tarrying, drink mine.

Oh! Ask the river flowing to the east, I pray,

If he is happier to go than I to stay!

夜下征虏亭[1]

船下广陵[2]去,
月明征虏亭。
山花如绣颊[3],
江火[4]似流萤。

[1]征虏亭:东晋时将军谢石所建,故址位于今江苏省南京市南郊。
[2]广陵:唐朝时,扬州别称。
[3]绣颊:涂过脂粉的女子面颊。
[4]江火:江上渔火。

　　船儿轻摇下扬州,皎皎明月照亮征虏古亭。月光下,山花绰约如少女,江上渔火似流萤。动亦静,静溢美,寥寥几笔,勾勒出一幅令人心醉的春江花月夜图景,悠游之乐显矣。

Passing by the Triumphal Tower at Night

My boat sails down to River Town,
The Tower's bright in the moonlight.
The flowers blow like cheeks that glow,
And lanterns beam as fireflies gleam.

上①李邕②

大鹏一日同风起,
扶③摇④直上九万里。
假令⑤风歇时下来,
犹能簸却⑥沧溟⑦水。
世人见我恒⑧殊调⑨,
闻余大言⑩皆冷笑。
宣父⑪犹能畏后生,
丈夫⑫未可轻年少。

①上：呈上。
②李邕：字泰和，广陵江都（今江苏江都）人。唐玄宗时任北海（今山东青州）太守，后被李林甫杀害。李邕长于李白，故诗题云"上"。
③扶：凭借。
④摇：由下而上的大风。
⑤假令：即使。
⑥簸却：激荡、激扬。
⑦沧溟：大海。
⑧恒：常常。
⑨殊调：格调特殊。
⑩大言：言谈自命不凡。
⑪宣父：孔子，唐太宗贞观年间诏尊孔子为宣父。
⑫丈夫：古代男子的通称，此处指李邕。

　　大鹏随风，扶摇直上九霄，无风仍能颠簸沧溟之水。世人见我如此大言，皆冷笑嘲讽。岂不知孔夫子亦曾言"后生可畏"，吾岁年少，未可轻视也！布衣李白直斥名士李邕，足见其自信和狂放！《庄子》的大鹏，是思想与灵魂自由的化身；

The Roc— to Li Yong

If once together with the wind the roc could rise,
He would fly ninety thousand miles up to the skies.
E'en if he must descend when the wind has abated,
Still billows will be raised and the sea agitated.
Seeing me, those in power think I'm rather queer;
Hearing me freely talk, they can't refrain from sneer.
Confucius was in dread of talents that would be;
A sage will ne'er look down upon a youth like me.

李白的大鹏是自己,是自由,是浪漫,更是直冲九霄的抱负!气度之浪漫与抱负之宏伟集于一身,古往今来,唯李白一人而已!此诗成于李白弱冠之时,少年英姿勃发,愿能如大鹏"扶摇直上九万里";其直到临终时,仍歌大鹏"余风激兮万世"。谪仙漫狂,一生不改!壮哉!

静夜思

床前明月光,
疑①是地上霜。
举②头望明月,
低头思故乡。

①疑:好像。
②举:抬。

    杰作一看就懂,但一看就懂的杰作往往最难写。好文字是挤压的产物,犹如钻石的硬与美。闯荡天地的李白初尝人世冷暖,又遭遇生病,百感交集,寂寂孤卧扬州旅舍。生命冲动受阻,强大者冲力更强。"举头望明月,低头思故乡",中国文学史上最能代表汉民族思乡情怀的诗句产生了,"水石相击,声如洪钟。"

Thoughts on a Silent Night

Before my bed a pool of light—
Is it hoarfrost upon the ground?
Eyes raised, I see the moon so bright;
Head bent, in homesickness I'm drowned.

黄鹤楼送孟浩然之①广陵

故人②西辞黄鹤楼,
烟花③三月下④扬州。
孤帆远影碧空尽,
唯见长江天际流。

①之:到达。
②故人:指孟浩然。
③烟花:形容柳絮如烟、鲜花盛开的春天景象。
④下:顺流而下。

  扬州三月,柳絮如烟,姹紫嫣红。孤帆、远影、长江、天际——孤帆已远,犹见天水一色;碧空千里,不胜依依。诗境如画境!诗句灵动飘逸、意境悠长!离别本伤怀,然烟花春色冲淡了这伤,诗中亦有孟夫子正为此绚烂春景下江南之意。此次别离充满了潇洒诗意,故而李白惜别意短,向往情长!

Seeing Meng Haoran off at Yellow Crane Tower

My friend has left the west where towers Yellow Crane
For River Town when willow-down and flowers reign.
His lessening sail is lost in boundless azure sky,
Where I see but the endless River rolling by.

长相思（二首其一）

长相思，
在长安。
络纬①秋啼金井阑②，
微霜凄凄簟③色寒。
孤灯不明思欲绝，
卷帷望月空长叹。
美人如花隔云端。
上有青冥之高天，
下有渌水之波澜。
天长地远魂飞苦，
梦魂不到关山难。
长相思，
摧心肝！

①络纬：虫名，即莎鸡，俗称络丝娘、纺织娘。
②金井阑：精美的井栏。
③簟：竹席。

自《离骚》以降，以美人喻君王，此诗更有"在长安"之语，可见此长相思是思君王之思。

诗中用亮色之词，如金、霜、青、渌等，凸显意境澄澈；复用五感之语，如啼、凄、寒、孤、绝、空、隔、苦、摧等，

Lovesickness (I)

I yearn for one

Who's in Chang'an

In autumn crickets wail beside the golden rail;

The first frost, although light, invades the bed's delight.

My lonely lamp burns dull, of longing I would die;

Rolling up screens to view the moon, in vain I sigh.

My flower-like Beauty is high

Up as clouds in the sky.

Above, the boundless heaven blue is seen;

Below, the endless river rolls its billows green.

My soul can't fly o'er sky so vast nor earth so wide;

In dreams I can't go through mountain pass to her side.

We are so far apart,

The yearning breaks my heart.

更显诗意清婉,凄恻动人。而"青冥高天""渌水波澜""天长地远""梦魂关山"之语,想象奇绝而广阔。虽求仕不成、相思成空,却不泄胸中浩然之气,此即为其诗魂动人心魄之处!

长相思（二首其二）

日色①欲尽花含烟②，
月明如素愁不眠。
赵瑟③初停凤凰柱④，
蜀琴欲奏鸳鸯弦。
此曲有意无人传，
愿随春风寄燕然。
忆君迢迢隔青天。
昔时横波目，
今作流泪泉。
不信妾肠断，
归来看取明镜前！

①日色：天色。
②烟：雾气。
③赵瑟：相传为古代赵国人，善弹瑟。瑟，弦乐器。
④凤凰柱：雕刻成凤凰状的瑟柱。

　　日色将尽，花含烟雾，明月如素，营造出忧伤氛围。赵瑟蜀琴，欲奏却无人传情，愿托春风寄思念。忆君隔青天，尽露相思之苦。昔日的美目今成泪泉，以夸张之法突显深情。末句不信肠断，待君归来鉴，更是强烈表达出女子的执着与哀怨，感情细腻真挚，令人动容。

Lovesickness (II)

Flowers exhale thin mist when daylight fades away;
The sleepless feel sad to see the moon shed silken ray.
My harp on phoenix-holder has just become mute,
I'll try to play upon lovebird strings of my lute.
My song's a message.
Who will carry it to you?
I'd ask spring wind to bear it up to the frontiers.
Between you and me there is the boundless blue sky.
Do you remember my wave-like eyes of days gone by?
Now they become a spring of tears.
If you do not believe my heart is broken, alas!
Come back and look into my bright mirror of brass!

登新平①楼

去国②登兹楼③,
怀归伤暮秋。
天长落日远,
水净寒波流。
秦云④起岭树,
胡雁⑤飞沙洲。
苍苍几万里,
目极⑥令人愁。

①新平：唐朝郡名，即邠州，治所在新平县（今陕西省彬县）。
②去国：离开国都。
③兹楼：指新平楼。兹，此。
④秦云：秦地的云。新平在先秦时属秦国。
⑤胡雁：北方的大雁。
⑥目极：望向远方。

　　踌躇满志闯长安却处处碰壁，失意而返的李白登上邠州新平楼，满目暮秋之景：落日远、寒波流、云起、雁飞——回望长安，多少复杂情绪涌上心头？愤懑、无奈、忧国、怀归……汇集成愁思万里，明伤秋，实伤人。飞扬跋扈又不失唯美伤感的气势，岂是一个"愁"字了得！

Ascending Xinping Tower

Leaving the capital, I climb this tower.
Can I return home like late autumn flower?
The sky is vast, the setting sun is far;
The water clear, the waves much colder are.
Clouds rise above the western-mountain trees;
O'er river dunes fly south-going wild geese.
The boundless land outspread 'neath gloomy skies.
How gloomy I feel while I strain my eyes!

辑二

长风破浪会有时

蜀道难

噫吁嚱[①],

危乎高哉!

蜀道之难,

难于上青天!

蚕丛及鱼凫[②],

开国何茫然!

尔来[③]四万八千岁,

不与秦塞通人烟。

西当太白[④]有鸟道[⑤],

可以横绝峨眉巅。

地崩山摧壮士死,

然后天梯石栈相钩连。

上有六龙回日之高标,

①噫吁嚱(xī):蜀方言,表示惊讶的声音。
②蚕丛、鱼凫(fú):皆是传说中的古蜀国国王。
③尔来:从那时以来。
④太白:山名,秦岭主峰,在今陕西省周至、太白县一带。
⑤鸟道:极言山路之险峻,仅能容鸟飞过。

《蜀道难》为乐府旧题,自李太白出,"难于上青天"为蜀道盖棺论定。首句"噫吁嚱,危乎高哉!蜀道之难,难于上青天!",明明是咏叹蜀道之难,字字读去却胸中豪情顿吐!紧接着声调渐缓,将蜀地历史一一道来。李白以雄奇之笔,将传说与蜀道奇伟天险结合,入蜀之艰险更添蜀地之神秘、传说之奇绝。鸟道、猿猱道皆非人能行,果然难于上青天!

Hard Is the Road to Shu

Oho! Behold!

How steep!

How high!

The road to Shu is harder than to climb to the sky.

Since the two pioneers

Put the kingdom in order,

Have passed forty-eight thousand years,

And few have tried to pass its border.

There's a bird track o'er Great White Mountain to the west,

Which cuts through Mountain Eyebrows by the crest.

The crest crumbled, five serpent-killing heroes slain,

Along the cliffs a rocky path was hacked then.

Above stand peaks too high for the sun to pass o'er;

太白峰、青泥岭、剑阁、锦城，又为西入蜀地路线，李白天马行空之思一丝不乱！且不忘提醒当政者"所守或匪亲，化为狼与豺"，自古艰险之地尤其容易成为割据要塞，可见李白济世之心须臾不忘！

全诗前中后三次咏叹"蜀道之难，难于上青天！"，回环往复激荡心怀！诗人笔意纵横豪迈，有一泻千里、滔滔不绝之势。

下有冲波逆折之回川。
黄鹤之飞尚不得过,
猿猱欲度愁攀援。
青泥何盘盘,
百步九折萦岩峦。
扪参历井⑥仰胁息⑦,
以手抚膺坐长叹。
问君西游何时还?
畏途巉岩⑧不可攀。
但见悲鸟号古木,
雄飞雌从绕林间。
又闻子规⑨啼夜月,
愁空山。
蜀道之难,
难于上青天,
使人听此凋朱颜⑩。
连峰去天不盈尺,
枯松倒挂倚绝壁。
飞湍⑪瀑流争喧豗⑫,
砯⑬崖转石万壑雷。
其险也如此,
嗟尔远道之人胡为乎来哉!

⑥扪(mén)参历井:参、井是二星宿名。古人把星宿分别对应州国,叫作"分野",以便通过观察天象来占卜所对应州国的吉凶。参星为蜀之分野,井星为秦之分野。扪,用手摸。历,经过。
⑦胁息:敛声屏气,不敢呼吸。
⑧巉(chán)岩:险峻陡峭的山壁。
⑨子规:杜鹃鸟。
⑩凋朱颜:红颜带有忧色,如花的凋零。
⑪飞湍:飞奔的急流。
⑫喧豗(huī):喧闹声,此处指瀑布发出的巨大声响。
⑬砯(pīng):水撞击石头发出的声音,此处作动词,撞击的意思。

Below the torrents run back and forth, churn and roar.
Even the Golden Crane can't fly across;
How to climb over, gibbons are at a loss.
What tortuous mountain path Green Mud Ridge faces!
Around the top we turn nine turns each hundred paces.
Looking up breathless, I can touch the stars nearby;
Beating my breast, I sink aground with long, long sigh.
When will you come back from this journey to the west?
How can you climb up dangerous path and mountain crest,
Where you can hear on ancient trees but sad birds wail
And see the female birds fly, followed by the male?
And hear home-going cuckoos weep
Beneath the moon in mountains deep?
The road to Shu is harder than to climb to the sky,
On hearing this, your cheeks would lose their rosy dye.
Between the sky and peaks there is not a foot's space,
And ancient pines hang, head down, from the cliff's surface,
And cataracts and torrents dash on boulders under,
Roaring like thousands of echoes of thunder.
So dangerous these places are,
Alas! Why should you come here from afar?

剑阁⑭峥嵘而崔嵬,
一夫当关,
万夫莫开。
所守⑮或匪亲,
化为狼与豺。
朝避猛虎,
夕避长蛇,
磨牙吮血,
杀人如麻。
锦城虽云乐,
不如早还家。
蜀道之难,难于上青天,
侧身西望长咨嗟⑯!

⑭剑阁:又名剑门关,位于四川省剑阁县北。
⑮所守:把守关口的人。
⑯咨嗟:叹息。

Rugged is the path between the cliffs so steep and high,

Guarded by one

And forced by none.

Disloyal guards

Would turn wolves and pards.

Man-eating tigers at daybreak

And at dusk blood-sucking long snake.

One may make merry in the Town of Silk, I know,

But I would rather homeward go.

The road to Shu is harder than to climb to the sky,

I'd turn and westward look with long, long sigh.

行路难（三首其一）

金樽清酒斗十千，
玉盘珍羞①直②万钱。
停杯投箸不能食，
拔剑四顾心茫然。
欲渡黄河冰塞川，
将登太行③雪满山。
闲来垂钓碧溪上，
忽复乘舟梦日边。
行路难，
行路难，
多歧路，
今安在？
长风破浪④会有时，
直挂云帆济⑤沧海。

①珍羞：名贵的菜肴。羞，同"馐"。
②直：同"值"。
③太行：太行山。
④长风破浪：比喻实现政治理想。
⑤济：渡。

　　金樽清酒、玉盘珍馐，"三杯通大道、一斗合自然"的李白，却停杯箸，食不甘味；拔剑起舞，却依旧满心茫然。"仰天大笑"入长安，不过两年，竟被"赐金放还"，仕途之阻隔，恰如冰塞黄河、雪满太行，山路水路都无路！然是否可学太公垂钓、伊尹梦日？噫！此路虽艰，歧路虽险，然未必不能

Hard Is the Way of the World (I)

Pure wine in golden cup costs ten thousand coppers, good!

Choice dish in a jade plate is worth as much, nice food!

Pushing aside my cup and chopsticks, I can't eat;

Drawing my sword and looking round, I stamp my feet.

I can't cross Yellow River: ice has stopped its flow;

I can't climb Mount Taihang: the sky is blind with snow.

I can but poise a fishing pole beside a stream

Or set sail for the sun like a sage in a dream.

Hard is the way,

Hard is the way.

Don't go astray!

Whither today?

A time will come to ride the wind and cleave the waves,

I'll set my cloud-white sail and cross the sea which raves.

有挂云帆乘长风破万里浪、横渡沧海之日！全诗想象奇绝，思绪跨越时空，读来韵律顿挫、心绪起伏，却又自然而适。

　　李白兼具浪漫与豪情。停杯投箸是文人低首，拔剑四顾却如侠士悲慨，悲愤至极，却又豪情满怀。此人风骨真能神游八极之表！全篇虽仿鲍照《拟行路难》，却意气豪放胜其远矣。

行路难（三首其二）

大道如青天，
我独不得出。
羞逐长安社①中儿，
赤鸡白狗②赌梨栗。
弹剑作歌③奏苦声，
曳裾王门不称情。
淮阴市井笑韩信，
汉朝公卿忌贾生④。
君不见，
昔时燕家重郭隗，
拥篲⑤折节无嫌猜。
剧辛乐毅感恩分，
输肝剖胆效英才。

①社：古代，二十五家为一社。
②白狗：一作"白雉"。
③弹剑作歌：战国时，齐国孟尝君门客冯谖曾屡次弹剑作歌感叹不如意，此处代指壮志难酬。
④贾生：指贾谊，西汉著名思想家。
⑤拥篲（huì）：手执笤帚扫地。古人迎候宾客，拥篲以示恭敬。后因用为典实。

行路难，仕途之路尤其难！历代贤达，功成而身不退者皆不得善终，何必追慕孤高之名。人生得意事，莫过一杯酒，前贤达人徒留虚名，于人生何意？不如及时归去，赏秋风秋意，品吴中菰菜鲈鱼！李白情怀自适，仕途遇阻，以前贤之例宽

Hard Is the Way of the World (II)

The way is broad like the blue sky,

But no way out before my eye.

I am ashamed to follow those who have no guts,

Gambling on fighting cocks and dogs for pears and nuts.

Feng would go homeward way, having no fish to eat;

Zhou did not think to bow to noblemen was meet.

General Han was mocked in the marketplace;

The brilliant scholar Jia was banished in disgrace.

Have you not heard of King of Yan in days gone by,

Who venerated talents and built Terrace high

On which he offered gold to gifted men

And stooped low and swept the floor to welcome them?

Grateful, Ju Xin and Yue Yi came then

And served him heart and soul, both full of stratagem.

慰自己，表达杯酒人生之念！全诗句句有典，可见其慰己自适之情切！然字里行间并无其一贯的潇洒快意，依旧有未达"海内清一"理想而不得不退身江湖的无奈，可见此诗只是一时之情绪抒发而已！

昭王白骨萦蔓草，
谁人更扫黄金台？
行路难，
归去来！⑥

⑥归去来：指隐居，语出陶渊明《归去来辞》。

The King's bones were now buried, who would sweep the floor

Of the Gold Terrace any more?

Hard is the way.

Go back without delay!

行路难（三首其三）

有耳莫洗颍川水①，
有口莫食首阳蕨②。
含光混世贵无名，
何用孤高比云月？
吾观自古贤达人，
功成不退皆殒身。
子胥③既弃吴江上，
屈原④终投湘水滨。
陆机⑤雄才岂自保？⑥
李斯⑦税驾苦不早。
华亭鹤唳讵可闻？
上蔡苍鹰何足道？

①"有耳"句：这句诗引用了尧时高士许由不受尧的官位，不愿听尧封官的话，而去洗耳的故事。
②首阳蕨：首阳山上的野菜。这里指的是伯夷、叔齐在首阳山采食的野菜。
③子胥：伍子胥，春秋末期吴国大夫。
④屈原：战国时期楚国诗人。
⑤陆机：西晋文学家。
⑥"陆机"句：《晋书·陆机传》载：陆机因宦人诬陷而被杀害于军中，临终叹曰："华亭鹤唳，岂可复闻乎？"
⑦李斯：秦朝宰相。

仕途无望，李白内心矛盾又挣扎。此诗以不效仿许由、伯夷叔齐开篇，表现了对功名利禄并非完全摒弃的复杂心绪。"含光混世"与"孤高比云月"对比，展现诗人在不同人生选择之间的纠结。诗人对现实无奈和反抗，以一种否定传统的方式来抒发内心的愤懑和对人生道路的迷茫。用子胥、屈原、

Hard Is the Way of the World (III)

Don't wash your ears on hearing something you dislike

Nor die of hunger like famous hermits on the Pike!

Living without high fame among the motley crowd,

Why should one be as lofty as the moon or cloud?

Of ancient talents who failed to retire, there's none

But came to tragic ending after glory's won.

The head of General Wu was hung o'er city gate;

In the river was drowned the Poet Laureate.

The highly talented scholar wished in vain

To preserve his life to hear the cry of the crane.

Minister Li regretted not to have retired

To hunt with falcon gray as he had long desired.

陆机、李斯等典故,道出贤达之士功成不退皆殒身的观点,充满历史的沉重感。接着以张翰及时行乐作结,一句"且乐生前一杯酒,何须身后千载名",诉说诗人无奈之下,对自由适意人生的向往。

君不见,
吴中张翰⁸称达生,
秋风忽忆江东行。
且乐生前一杯酒,
何须身后千载名?

⑧张翰:西晋文学家。

Have you not heard of Zhang Han who resigned, carefree,

To go home to eat his perch with high glee?

Enjoy a cup of wine while you're alive!

Do not care if your fame will not survive!

送友人入蜀

见说^①蚕丛路,
崎岖不易行。
山从人面起,
云傍马头生。
芳树笼秦栈^②,
春流绕蜀城^③。
升沉^④应已定,
不必问君平^⑤。

①见说:听说。
②秦栈:由秦入蜀的栈道。
③蜀城:成都。
④升沉:指功名得失。
⑤君平:严遵,字君平,西汉蜀郡(今四川)人。他喜好老庄思想,隐居不仕,在成都以占卜为生。

诗一开篇,李白先言蜀道崎岖不易行。接着以"山从人面起,云傍马头生",极言蜀道之险峻,落笔细腻,画面感十足。而后"芳树笼秦栈,春流绕蜀城",又描绘出蜀地的秀丽风光。末句既有对友人的宽慰,又流露出一种豁达的人生态度。整首诗既展现了蜀道之难,又有对友人的祝福,情感真挚,意境开阔。

To a Friend Departing for Shu

Rugg'd is the road, I hear,

Built by the pioneer.

In front steep mountains rise;

Beside the steed cloud flies.

O'er plank-way trees hang down;

Spring water girds the town.

Decid'd our rise and fall,

Do not bother at all!

春夜洛城①闻笛

谁家玉笛暗飞声？
散入东风满洛城。
此夜曲中闻《折柳》②，
何人不起故园情？

①洛城：今河南省洛阳市。
②《折柳》：《折杨柳》笛曲，多写离情别绪。

    洛城春夜，风吹笛声散满城，隐隐听到《折柳》曲，惹动思乡之情。李白求仕不成，客居洛阳。羌笛古曲有《折杨柳》，李白知音识曲，妙思万千，"谁家""何人"，皆有心人也。一"暗"字点明羁旅客愁之人方能听到此曲，然有吹奏者，有听者，其乡愁亦如此曲随风飘散，万千愁思笼罩满城。此景诗意而浪漫，此情婉转而悠扬。

Hearing a Bamboo Flute on a Spring Night in Luoyang

From whose house comes the voice of flute of jade unseen?
It fills the town of Luoyang, spread by wind of spring.
Tonight I hear the farewell song of Willows Green.
To whom the tune will not nostalgic feeling bring?

塞下曲（六首其一）

五月天山①雪，
无花只有寒。
笛中闻《折柳》，
春色未曾看。
晓战随金鼓，
宵眠抱玉鞍。
愿将腰下剑，
直为斩楼兰。

①天山：祁连山。

　　盛夏五月，天山仍飞雪，无花只有寒，以直白淡然之语写尽边地苦寒。战士们只能听《折柳》之曲，却不见柳絮如烟、繁花春景。不论晓夜，战士皆抱鞍而眠，闻金鼓之鸣即刻出战，拔出腰下长剑，破胡虏保天下平安！诗句全无雕饰，只将天山、无花、寒、金鼓、鞍、剑、楼兰此等边塞之象征连缀，竟成雄浑豪迈之诗！苦寒之地与烟柳花香，听曲思乡与金鼓战袍，战士们身处绝地，身有柔肠而不改英勇豪壮，真大唐之魂也！大唐之魂与诗人之笔，皆若神赐也！

Frontier Song (I)

In summer sky-high mountains white with snow,
In bitter cold no fragrant flowers blow.
Songs on the flute are heard of Willows Green,
But nowhere is the vernal color seen.
From dawn till dusk to beats of drum they fight;
With saddle in their arms they rest at night.
From scabbard at my waist I'd draw my sword
To kill the chieftain of the Turki horde.

关山月①

明月出天山,
苍茫云海间。
长风几万里,
吹度玉门关②。
汉下③白登道,
胡窥④青海湾。
由来征战地,
不见有人还。
戍客⑤望边色,
思归多苦颜。
高楼当此夜,
叹息未应闲。

①关山月：乐府旧题，多抒发离别之情。
②玉门关：故址位于今甘肃省敦煌西北，古代通向西域的交通要道。
③下：指出兵。
④窥：窥探、侵扰。
⑤戍客：戍守边疆的士兵。

  明月、天山、云海、长风、几万里，勾勒出边塞之地的辽阔苍凉。仰望云天，苍茫高渺；回望关山，家乡万里。这征战之地便是埋骨之所，妻子家乡只在梦里。唯有明月照见千年、万里，照见戍客怀乡思妇断肠，照见两地相思千古之伤。盛唐威武，犹有戍客望关山、思妇高楼上。边界冲突千年不断，百代人的牺牲让这相思悲壮而深沉！诗人无一字言"止战"，却句句不离征战苦！千百年来多少戍客思妇的血和泪，才换来今日的和平！珍惜！珍惜！

The Moon over the Mountain Pass

From Heaven's Peak the moon rises bright,
Over a boundless sea of cloud.
Winds blow for miles with main and might
Past the Jade Gate which stands so proud.
Our warriors march down the frontier
While Tartars peer across Blue Bays.
From the battlefield outstretched here,
None have come back since olden days.
Guards watch the scene of borderland,
Thinking of home, with wistful eyes.
Tonight upstairs their wives would stand,
Looking afar with longing sighs.

乌夜啼[1]

黄云城边乌欲栖,
归飞哑哑枝上啼。
机中织锦[2]秦川女[3],
碧纱如烟隔窗语。
停梭怅然忆远人[4],
独宿孤房泪如雨。

[1]乌夜啼:乐府旧题,多抒发男女相思之苦。
[2]机中织锦:指闺中织妇。
[3]秦川女:指晋朝苏蕙,此处泛指织锦女子。
[4]远人:指远在外地的丈夫。

　　这原是一幅隽永的归巢图:落日余晖下云层染金,大树上乌鸦归巢,屋舍内机杼声声。啼乌归巢声惊动织妇,停梭隔窗而望。窗外是哑哑啼叫的归鸟,热闹而温馨;窗内却是良人久不回,孤影伴孤魂。织妇怅然自语,凄然泪下。诗中借前秦才女苏蕙写思妇闺怨。今之织妇不如苏蕙才情卓绝,思夫之情、坚贞之念却不减才女分毫。李白以"心雄万夫"的男儿身,是在为古今天下的女子发声!

The Crows Crying at Night

'Neath yellow clouds the crows fly home by city wall,
They caw amid the leaves in treetops at night-fall.
The wife of Western Plain weaves brocade at her loom,
Behind the misty screen she murmurs — but to whom?
She stops her shuttle, thinking of him far away,
And weeps, so lonely in her bower night and day.

春思

燕草①如碧丝,
秦桑②低绿枝。
当君③怀归④日,
是妾断肠时。
春风不相识,
何事入罗帏⑤?

① 燕草:燕地的草。燕,河北省北部,此处指征夫所在之处。
② 秦桑:秦地的桑树。秦,陕西省一带,此处指思妇所在之地。
③ 君:指征夫。
④ 怀归:想家。
⑤ 罗帏:丝质的帘帐。

  这是一场春天的情思。起句以"丝"谐"思",以"枝"谐"知"——我在秦地思你念你你可知?次句貌似无理,然则为思之刻骨,言"君方起念妾已断肠";末句余味无穷,春风撩人频掀罗帏,却斥之不相识,其专情若揭!太白攫倚天之剑摹思妇之思,洞察女性之细腻、婉转、幽微,浑然一体。思妇之长情、专情,倒衬出网络时代的寡情了。

A Faithful Wife Longing for Her Husband in Spring

Your Northern grass must be like green silk thread;

Our Western mulberries have bent their head.

When your thoughts begin to turn homeward way,

My heart has long been breaking night and day.

To the intruding vernal wind I say:

"How dare you part the curtain of my bed!"

三五七言[①]

秋风清,
秋月明。
落叶聚还散,
寒鸦栖复惊。
相思相见知何日?
此时此夜难为情!

[①]三五七言:一种诗歌体裁。全诗三言、五言、七言各两句,故名。

　　三五七言诗体独特地位的确立应归功于李太白,此诗为源头。秋风、秋月、落叶、寒鸦,一派萧瑟悲凉之景,言浅而哀浓。太白究竟写谁呢?写自己思家念亲还是代闺中思妇抒怀?诗人内在的情绪决定了语言的节奏与形态。也罢,相思漫卷似潮涌,凄清孤寂夜难寝——世人皆当有此情吧!

Yearning

Fresh autumn breeze,

Bright autumn moon.

Fallen leaves gather and scatter around the trees;

Cold-stricken crows soon fall asleep and wake as soon.

I long for you. When can I see your longing look?

How can I bear this lonely night, this lonely nook?

怨情

美人卷珠帘,
深坐颦①蛾眉②。
但看泪痕湿,
不知心恨谁。

①颦:皱眉。
②蛾眉:美人的眉毛,也喻指美女。

  李白小时候就向往司马相如,向往谢安,伏下他对美色的敏感。提笔一挥,三言两语刻画美人之幽怨情态,入木三分。懒卷珠帘,深坐颦眉,泪湿见其恨深,但妙就妙在"不知"——美人不知自己是爱是恨,旁人不知美人源何爱恨。见其态而难闻其详更惹遐思无数……

Waiting in Vain

A lady fair uprolls the screen,
With eyebrows knit she waits in vain.
Wet stains of tears can still be seen.
Who, heartless, has caused her the pain?

玉阶怨[1]

玉阶生白露,
夜久侵罗袜[2]。
却下水晶帘,
玲珑望秋月。

[1]玉阶怨:乐府古题,专写"宫怨"主题。
[2]罗袜:丝质的袜子。

宫禁深深,爱一个人、盼一个人究竟能起多少相思?等到白露生,痴到秋月怜。月且伴人,人则谁伴?似脱口而出的透明纯净,读来口齿生香余韵悠长,然则想来却有彻骨之寒、之怜。全诗不著一"怨"字,而幽怨弥漫千古,深,深!

Waiting in Vain on Marble Steps

The marble steps with dew turn cold,
Silk soles are wet when night grows old.
She comes in, lowers crystal screen,
Still gazing at the moon serene.

长门怨① (二首其一)

天回北斗②挂西楼,
金屋无人萤火流。
月光欲到长门殿,
别作深宫一段愁。

①长门怨:古乐府诗题。
②天回北斗:北斗七星。

Sorrow of the Long Gate Palace (I)

The plough has turned around and hangs o'er Western Tower,
None but the fireflies sail the gloom of Golden Bower.
The lonely moon which peeps in Palace of Long Gate
Will shed more sorrow on the dweller desolate.

长门怨（二首其二）

桂殿[1]长愁不记春[2],
黄金四屋[3]起秋尘。
夜悬明镜[4]青天上,
独照长门宫里人。

①桂殿：长门殿。
②不记春：不记得是哪一年，言时间之长。
③四屋：四壁。
④明镜：指月亮。

　　司马相如为陈皇后作《长门赋》，后人因其赋而为《长门怨》。此诗据载写于太白长安待诏翰林之时，当是借这一旧题来泛写宫人的愁怨。

　　唐朝皇宫中宫女数量为各朝之冠，玄宗时期尤多，多少如花生命在寂寞深宫里摧折、凋零、朽腐！如果说《玉阶怨》尚觉一颗年轻的心跳，《长门怨》则死寂如潭，任春风吹不起涟漪。金屋堂皇却秋尘四布，道不尽这似海深愁，连阅人间百态无情的月光也似染了尘心，不忍照而无法不照，更添清冷。

　　千红一窟，万艳同杯。谁为女性发声？[1]

----

[1]《长门怨》（二首其一）和《长门怨》（二首其二）合并赏析。

Sorrow of the Long Gate Palace (II)

Does Laurel Bower where grief reigns remember spring?
On the four golden walls the dusts of autumn cling.
The night holds up a mirror bright in azure sky
To show the fair on earth as lonely as on high.

子夜吴歌①（春歌）

秦地②罗敷女③，
采桑绿水边。
素手青条上，
红妆白日鲜。
蚕饥妾欲去，
五马莫留连④！

①子夜吴歌：乐府的吴声曲辞。又名《子夜四时歌》。
②秦地：指今陕西省关中地区。
③罗敷女：乐府诗《陌上桑》有"日出东南隅，归我秦氏楼。秦氏有好女，自名为罗敷。罗敷善蚕桑，采桑城南隅"的诗句。
④"五马"句：意即，达官贵人莫要在此留连。五马，《汉官仪》记载："四马载车，此常礼也，惟太守出，则增一马。"故称五马。此处指达官贵人。

  陶渊明《四时诗》云："春水满四泽，夏云多奇峰。秋月扬明晖，冬岭秀孤松。"古人对四季是极为敏感的，每个季节有不同的风物，也有不同的风情。李太白的《子夜吴歌》四首是借鉴民歌《子夜歌》而有所变化与发展，将春之明媚、夏之浓艳、秋之素洁、冬之寒冷与女性的典型活动相结合，为千年后的我们泼染四时画卷。

Ballads of Four Seasons（Spring）

The lovely Lo Fo of the western land

Plucks mulberry leaves by the waterside.

Across the green boughs stretches out her white hand;

In golden sunshine her rosy robe is dyed.

"My silkworms are hungry, I cannot stay.

Tarry not with your five-horse cab, I pray."

春歌改编自秦罗敷的故事：少女采桑绿水边，晴日红妆逼人眼，富贵王侯起色心，蚕饥自去不留连！好个不慕权贵的可爱女子，青葱美丽而又率真张扬，带着李白似的自由奔放——恰是锋芒毕露的青春！

子夜吴歌（夏歌）

镜湖①三百里，
菡萏②发荷花。
五月西施采，
人看隘若耶③。
回舟不待月，
归去越王④家！

①镜湖：一名鉴湖，位于今浙江绍兴市东南。
②菡（hàn）萏（dàn）：荷花的别称。
③若耶：指若耶溪，位于今浙江省绍兴市境内。
④越王：指越王勾践。

　　夏歌吟咏美女西施：广阔镜湖，荷花竞放；西施采莲，人人争睹——花美还是人美？美压三百里荷花！然而仅仅美还不够，太白接着写道：西施往哪回？归去越王家！为何不是吴王家？这是将娇美化为壮美，舍身取义为国复仇才是西施——夏之勃发与浓烈喷薄而出。

Ballads of Four Seasons（Summer）

On Mirror Lake outspread for miles and miles,
The lotus lilies in full blossom teem.
In fifth moon Xi Shi gathers them with smiles,
Watchers o'erwhelm the bank of Yoya Stream.
Her boat turns back without waiting moonrise
To royal house amid amorous sighs.

子夜吴歌（秋歌）

长安一片月，
万户捣衣①声。
秋风吹不尽，
总是玉关②情。
何日平③胡虏④？
良人⑤罢远征！

①捣衣：洗衣服时，将衣服放在砧石上用棒捶打。
②玉关：玉门关。
③平：平定。
④胡虏：侵扰边疆的敌人。
⑤良人：指驻守边疆的丈夫。

秋歌以月亮起兴：月夜清辉洒人间，万户捣衣声不绝——无数征夫之妇在忙着为戍边的丈夫制衣；下句由景转情，想象奇绝：浓浓相思秋风吹不尽，只好将寸寸相思捣入征衣送到边关；末句是万千呐喊：何时方能平敌寇，天下良人得还家？场景宏大而又柔婉，闻声而见人，见人而知情，情景交融，一片神韵。

Ballads of Four Seasons (*Autumn*)

Moonlight is spread all o'er the capital,

The sound of beating clothes far and near

Is brought by autumn wind which can't blow all

The longings away for far-off frontier.

When can we vanquish the barbarian foe

So that our men no longer into battle go?

子夜吴歌（冬歌）

明朝驿使①发，
一夜絮征袍。
素手抽针冷，
那堪把剪刀！
裁缝寄远道，
几日到临洮②？

①驿使：驿馆里负责传送文件的人员。
②临洮：位于今甘肃省定西市，此处泛指边地。

　　春采桑，夏采莲，秋捣衣，冬呢？冬絮袍。征衣还不够啊，一听到有驿使要去丈夫的戍地，赶紧熬夜絮件厚袍，不怕那抽针冷，不顾那剪刀冰。天明给驿使，连问几时成。没有冬景只有叙事，字字无奇却字字促逼，凸显一个"赶"。因"赶"，思妇形象呼之欲出。而冬的冷凛、冬的含蓄、冬的坚韧都在这个"赶"的思妇身上淋漓尽致地呈现出来。

　　春歌、夏歌、秋歌、冬歌，唐诗宋词背后是大规模的红颜贡献。

Ballads of Four Seasons (*Winter*)

The courier will depart next day, she's told,

She sews a warrior's gown all night.

Her fingers feel the needle cold.

How can she hold the scissors tight?

The work is done, she sends it far away.

When will it reach the town where warriors stay?

辑三

与尔同销万古愁

将进酒[1]

君不见[2]黄河之水天上来,
奔流到海不复回!
君不见高堂[3]明镜悲白发,
朝如青丝[4]暮成雪!
人生得意须尽欢,
莫使金樽空对月。
天生我材必有用,
千金散尽还复来。
烹羊宰牛且为乐,
会须[5]一饮三百杯。

[1]将进酒:属乐府旧题。
[2]君不见:乐府诗中常用的一种夸语。
[3]高堂:房屋的正室厅堂。此处指父母。
[4]青丝:黑发。
[5]会须:正应当。

此系李白代表作之一。生命冲动受阻,越发奔腾咆哮,一泻千里。李白写黄河,更是写生存的激流;李白写醉酒,更是写平生行路难,人世苦短而容颜易老。宋人严羽评点这首诗云:"一往豪情,使人不能句字赏摘,盖他人作诗用笔想,太白但用胸气一喷即是。"是的,"一喷即是"——诗人生命的冲动以酒为助推,如挟天风海雨扑面而来,轻易引人跃入

Invitation to Wine

Do you not see the Yellow River come from the sky,
Rushing into the sea and ne'er come back?
Do you not see the mirrors bright in chambers high
Grieve o'er your snow-white hair though once it was silk-black?
When hopes are won, oh! Drink your fill in high delight,
And never leave your wine cup empty in moonlight!
Heaven has made us talents, we're not made in vain.
A thousand gold coins spent, more will turn up again.
Kill a cow, cook a sheep and let us merry be,
And drink three hundred cupfuls of wine in high glee!

奔涌跌宕的情感激流,大起大落,大落大起……如椽巨笔构筑起惊心动魄的艺术力量,失意也被渲染如烈火烹油,一颗诗心自由奔放、淋漓尽致,尽显诗人桀骜不驯之态——这就是我们认识的李白!

岑夫子⑥,
丹丘生⑦,
将进酒,
杯莫停。

与君⑧歌一曲,
请君为我侧耳听。
钟鼓⑨馔玉⑩不足贵,
但愿长醉不复醒。
古来圣贤皆寂寞,
惟有饮者留其名。
陈王⑪昔时宴平乐⑫,
斗酒十千恣⑬欢谑。
主人何为言少钱,
径须⑭沽⑮取对君酌。
五花马⑯,
千金裘,
呼儿将出换美酒,
与尔同销⑰万古愁。

⑥岑夫子:岑勋。
⑦丹丘生:元丹丘。和岑夫子二人均为李白好友。
⑧与君:给你们,为你们。
⑨钟鼓:宴会时奏乐使用的乐器。
⑩馔(zhuàn)玉:形容食物像玉一样精美。
⑪陈王:指陈思王曹植。
⑫平乐:观名。在洛阳西门外,为汉代达官显贵的娱乐场所。
⑬恣:纵情恣意。
⑭径须:只管。
⑮沽:买。
⑯五花马:指名贵的骏马。
⑰销:同"消"。

Dear friends of mine,

Cheer up, cheer up!

I invite you to wine.

Do not put down your cup!

I will sing you a song, please hear,

O hear! Lend me a willing ear!

What difference will rare and costly dishes make?

I only want to get drunk and never to wake.

How many great men were forgotten through the ages?

But great drinkers are more famous than sober sages.

The Prince of Poets feast'd in his palace at will,

Drank wine at ten thousand a cask and laughed his fill.

A host should not complain of money he is short,

To drink with you I will sell things of any sort.

My fur coat worth a thousand coins of gold

And my flower-dappled horse may be sold

To buy good wine that we may drown the woe age-old.

赠孟浩然

吾爱孟夫子①,
风流天下闻。
红颜②弃轩冕③,
白首④卧松云⑤。
醉月频中圣⑥,
迷花⑦不事君⑧。
高山⑨安可仰?
徒此揖清芬⑩。

①孟夫子:指孟浩然。夫子,尊称。
②红颜:青年,此处指青年时代。
③轩冕:指官位爵禄。
④白首:白头,指老年时代。
⑤卧松云:指隐居。
⑥"醉月"句:月下饮酒。中圣,"中圣人"的简称。《三国志·魏书·徐邈传》记载,汉末,禁酒甚严。当时人讳说酒字,把清酒称为圣人,浊酒称为贤人。尚书郎徐邈私自饮酒,对人说是"中圣人"。后遂以"中圣人"或"中圣"称酒醉。
⑦迷花:迷恋花草。
⑧事君:侍奉皇帝。
⑨高山:言孟浩然品格高尚,如高山一般,令人敬仰。
⑩"徒此"句:只有在此向您高尚的人品致敬了。

To Meng Haoran

Dear Master Meng, I hail you from the heart,
Of your high value all the world is proud.
Red-cheek'd, from cap to cab you kept apart;
White-haired, you lie beneath the pine and cloud.
Drunken with wine as oft as with moonlight,
You love the blooms too much to serve the crown.
Of lofty mountain how to reach the height?
We can but breathe your fragrance the wind brings down.

这爱的宣言，在古代诗词中也唯有李太白了吧。首联开门见山，表达对孟浩然的钦敬爱慕之情，盛赞其"风流"之性。且看如何"风流"？弃仕取隐，把酒临风，好不潇洒自性！一红颜一白首，一醉一迷，夫子之不慕名利、行云流水般自由形象跃然。尾联再抒崇仰之态，要"一揖清芬"，几乎五体投地。全诗围绕"爱"字，首尾呼应，自然古朴，年轻诗人率真之情似汩汩流泉，只不知已近不惑的孟夫子如何回应这炽烈爱心？

夜泊牛渚[①]怀古

牛渚西江[②]夜,
青天无片云。
登舟望秋月,
空忆谢将军[③]。
余亦能高咏,
斯人[④]不可闻。
明朝挂帆席,
枫叶落纷纷。

①牛渚:山名,位于今安徽省马鞍山市西南。
②西江:古称从南京以西到江西境内的一段长江为西江,牛渚在西江一段。
③谢将军:东晋谢尚,今河南省太康县人,时任镇西将军。
④斯人:指谢将军。

《晋书·文苑传》记载:袁宏少时孤贫,以运租为业。镇西将军谢尚镇守牛渚,秋夜乘月泛江,听到袁宏在运租船上吟咏他自己的咏史诗,非常赞赏,于是邀宏过船谈论,直至天明。袁宏得到谢尚的赞誉,从此声名大著。对于失意的李白来说,这是现实中求而不得的幻想。知音难遇,空余年华逝去。"青天""秋月"描空阔辽远之境,"空忆""不可闻""枫叶落纷纷"现寂寞凄清之情——月夜泊牛渚,斯人独憔悴。

Thoughts on Old Time from
a Night-Mooring near Cattle Hill

I moor near Cattle Hill at night

When there's no cloud to fleck the sky.

On deck I gaze at the moon so bright,

Thinking of General Xie with a sigh.

I too can chant — to what avail?

None has like him a listening ear.

Tomorrow I shall hoist my sail,

'Mid fallen maple leaves I'll leave here.

客中^①行

兰陵^②美酒郁金香^③,
玉碗盛来琥珀^④光。
但使主人能醉客,
不知何处是他乡。

①客中:指旅居他乡。
②兰陵:今山东省临沂市兰陵县兰陵镇。
③郁金香:郁金的香气。郁金,其块根主要用为药材,亦可浸酒、染色。
④琥珀:一种树脂化石,呈黄色或赤褐色。这里形容美酒色泽如琥珀。

羁旅之作大多抒其"客愁",此诗却以美酒醇香、光泽潋滟之象绘出盛唐时期财阜物美的繁荣之境,似乎诗人早已沉醉此间"乐不思蜀"。对这样的李白来说,没有他乡,所到之处皆是故乡。而兰陵也因李白此诗盛名于大唐,成为美酒之都,其美酒文化传承至今。

While Journeying

How flavorous is golden-tuliped Lanling wine!
Filling my bowl of jade, in amber it will glow.
It is enough if you can make me drunk, host mine
No more nostalgia in foreign land shall I know.

陌上赠美人

骏马骄①行踏落花,
垂鞭直拂五云车②。
美人一笑褰③珠箔④,
遥指红楼是妾家。

①骄:指骏马的高大健壮。
②五云车:传说中神仙的座驾,此处指华丽的车驾。
③褰(qiān):掀起。
④珠箔:缀有珠子的车帘。

此无疑为一首艳情诗,要被王安石的"道德厌恶"指鼻子骂的。马骏实为人俊,五云车乃仙人所乘,喻美人之风姿卓然。最美的时节、最美的地点,公子美人相遇。"直拂"是有意还是有误且不论,美人这"一笑""遥指"真真惹人遐思。"邂逅相遇,适我愿兮"是《诗经》里的怦然心动,此诗似化此而成。艳则艳矣,然诗人故意用第三人称,马上公子谁得似?一笑。

To a Fair Lady Encountered on the Road

I trample fallen flowers on a steed so proud,

And flick my whip at a cab of five-colored cloud.

The jewelled curtain drawn reveals a lady fair.

Smiling, she points to a mansion red, "My house is there."

登太白峰[1]

西上太白峰,
夕阳穷登攀。
太白[2]与我语,
为我开天关[3]。
愿乘泠风[4]去,
直出浮云间。
举手可近月,
前行若无山。
一别武功[5]去,
何时复更还?

[1] 太白峰：太白山。
[2] 太白：指太白金星,此处指神仙。
[3] 天关：古星名,此处指想象中通天的门。
[4] 泠风：轻微的风。
[5] 武功：武功县。

"太白何苍苍,星辰上森列,去天三百里,邈尔与世绝。"太白山很高,但李白这一次却化实以虚：太白星可与之密语,通天的门可打开,御风而行可,上天揽月也可——飘飘然似羽化而登仙。何其曼妙！世俗无趣,不如入道飞升。然而,诗人似又并不甘心全然抛开世俗,于是自问：一别武功去,何时复更还？毕竟渴望有所作为始终萦绕于心无法释怀。浪漫与现实并非硬币的两面可以割裂,人生耐人寻味。

Ascending the Snow-White Peak

Ascending from the west the Peak Snow-White,

Not till the sun goes down I reach its height.

The snow-white Morning Star tells me to wait

Until he opens the Celestial Gate.

I wish to ride cold wind and floating cloud

To touch the moon and dwarf all mountains proud.

But once I left behind the Western land,

Could I return to the summit where I stand?

登广武①古战场怀古

秦鹿②奔野草,
逐之若飞蓬③。
项王④气盖世,
紫电明双瞳⑤。
呼吸⑥八千人,
横行起江东。
赤精斩白帝,
叱咤入关中。
两龙⑦不并跃,
五纬⑧与天同。
楚灭无英图,
汉兴有成功。

①广武:古城名。
②鹿:指帝位。
③飞蓬:一种植物。常随风旋转,故名飞蓬。
④项王:项羽。
⑤双瞳:两个瞳孔。传说项羽的眼珠有两个瞳孔。
⑥呼吸:一呼即来。
⑦两龙:指刘邦和项羽。
⑧五纬:指金木水火土五行。

  登临古战场,思接千载魂悠悠。刘邦项羽楚汉对峙,留下一生是非功过任后人评说。每个人心中都有一个刘邦,也都有一个项羽,哪怕历史早有公论——这就是文学的魅力。此诗兼叙事与抒情,夹叙夹议,赞扬刘邦兼有豪杰和圣人的气质,只有以这样的豪圣才能完成治平乱世统一天下的大任,又岂是俗儒阮籍能鄙薄的。李白一生蓄足了劲,无数次冲向

Reflections on the Ancient Battlefield at Guangwu

The Emperor of Qin had lost his deer,
And heroes chased it as thistle-down flies.
The Prince of Chu was brave without a peer,
With purple flashes in double-pupiled eyes.
He called eight thousand Southern youths to fight,
From eastern River shore they swept the foes.
The Duke of Han had killed the Serpent white,
And breaking through the Pass, his war cries rose.
Two rival Dragons reigned not at same time,
And five propitious stars appeared on high.
Chu perished for lack of ideal sublime;
The Duke expanded his realm beneath the sky.

权贵,要大干一番事业,要"寰宇大定,海县清一",奈何这样的志向终究只是个梦想!他无法成为豪圣。全诗人物形象鲜明,评论有理有据,一派洒脱超逸之气。

按剑清八极,
归酣歌《大风》。
伊昔临广武,
连兵决雌雄。
分我一杯羹,
太皇乃汝翁。
战争有古迹,
壁垒颓层穹。
猛虎啸洞壑,
饥鹰鸣秋空。
翔云列晓阵,
杀气赫长虹。
拨乱⑨属豪圣,
俗儒安可通?
沉湎呼竖子,
狂言非至公。
抚掌黄河曲,
嗤嗤⑩阮嗣宗⑪。

⑨拨乱：治平乱世。
⑩嗤嗤：嗤笑。
⑪阮嗣宗：阮籍。

He cleared eight borders with the sword he did wield,
And came back drunk and sang The Great Wind Song .
His army once came to this battlefield,
And fought the Prince to see who was the strong.
His father, captured, would be boiled alive,
"My father's yours, " he said, "in weal and woe."
Of ancient war few relics still survive,
The ramparts crumble to mounds high and low.
Fierce growling tigers fill the caves with dismay,
And hungry eagles cleave the autumn sky.
The morning clouds still make a battle array,
And war cries seem to pelt the rainbow on high.
To end disorder is the deed of sage.
Pedantic scholar, how dare you declare,
Drunken, the Duke was fellow of village?
You're mad and frenzy, unjust and unfair.
I clap my hands in view of this battleground,
And laugh away your ignorance profound.

南陵①别儿童入京

白酒新熟山中归,
黄鸡啄黍秋正肥。
呼童烹鸡酌白酒,
儿女嬉笑牵人衣。
高歌取醉欲自慰,
起舞落日争光辉②。
游说万乘③苦不早,
著鞭跨马涉远道。
会稽愚妇轻买臣,
余亦辞家西入秦④。
仰天大笑出门去,
我辈岂是蓬蒿人⑤?

①南陵:一说在东鲁,曲阜县南陵城村,称为南陵;一说在今安徽省南陵县。
②"起舞"句:指人逢喜事精神焕发,与日光相辉映。
③万乘(shèng):君主。周朝制度,天子地方千里,车万乘。后以"万乘"代指皇帝。
④秦:指长安。春秋战国时期为秦地。
⑤蓬蒿人:民间百姓,即没有当官的人。蓬、蒿,都是植物,此处代指民间。

天宝元年(742),李白终于得召要进京了。如此人生大事,且看诗人如何挥洒满腔得意与踌躇满志:从酒熟秋肥入笔展欢愉之情;烹鸡酌酒、儿女牵衣、高歌痛饮、纵情舞剑,几个场景再描兴奋之态;"苦不早"与"轻买臣"更是压抑不住地扬眉吐气、志得意满,正所谓:青云直上指日待,人生得意须尽欢!但这还不够,至结尾,李太白振臂高呼"仰天

Parting from My Children at Nanling for the Capital

I come to hillside home when wine is newly brewed,

And yellow chicken feed on grains which autumn's strewed.

I call my lad to boil the fowl and pour the wine,

My children tug me by the sleeve, their faces shine.

I sing away to show my joy when wine is drunk;

I dance to vie in splendor with the sun half sunk.

Though it is late to offer service to the crown,

Still I will spur my horse on my way to renown.

The silly wife despised the talent not yet blest,

I'll leave my family and journey to the west.

Looking up at the sky, I laugh aloud and go.

Am I a man to crawl amid the brambles low?

大笑出门去，我辈岂是蓬蒿人"，将翻波涌浪的诗情推至顶点，也为我们的民族文化留下了个人自信与豪迈的根基。

清平调词（三首其一）

云想衣裳花想容，
春风拂槛①露华浓②。
若非群玉③山头见，
会向瑶台月下逢。

①槛：栏杆。
②露华浓：牡丹花沾着露水，更显浓艳。
③群玉：山名，传说是西王母的住所。

The Beautiful Lady Yang (I)

Her face is seen in flower and her dress in cloud,

A beauty by the rails caressed by vernal breeze.

If not a Fairy Queen from Jade-Green Mountains proud,

She's Goddess of the Moon in Crystal Hall one sees.

清平调词（三首其二）

一枝红艳露凝香，
云雨巫山枉断肠。
借问汉宫谁得似①？
可怜飞燕②倚新妆。

①得似：相似。
②飞燕：赵飞燕，西汉皇后。

The Beautiful Lady Yang (II)

She is a peony sweetened by dew impearled,
Far fairer than the Goddess bringing showers in dreams.
Who could equal her in palace of ancient world?
Not e'en the newly-dressed "Flying Swallow", it seems.

清平调词（三首其三）

名花^①倾国^②两相欢，
长得君王带笑看。
解释^③春风无限恨，
沉香亭^④北倚阑干。

①名花：指牡丹花。
②倾国：指杨贵妃。
③解释：消散。
④沉香亭：亭子名，位于唐长安城兴庆宫内龙池东北方。

李白这三首小诗，历来被视为绝唱。他四十二岁到长安做翰林供奉，写了很多诗歌颂帝王，一首佳作都没有，只留下一些可作史料看的"诗证"。写杨玉环却是字字佳：云想她的衣裳花想她的容貌，名花牡丹倾城倾国，君王看不够。究竟是君王看不够还是李白看不够呢？杨玉环又是激情澎湃的舞蹈家，谁堪比呢？汉宫能作掌上舞的赵飞燕。杨妃偏胖，"肥到杨妃肉亦佳"，赵飞燕瘦玲珑，李白拿杨妃比飞燕，全不考虑胖瘦问题。诗人态度，颇具轩昂。贵妃荣华造极也，何以

The Beautiful Lady Yang (III)

The lady fair admires and is admired by the flower,
The sovereign would gaze upon her with a smile.
She leans on balustrade north of the Fragrant Bower,
The longing of spring wind she knows how to beguile.

在春风中有无限恨？恨什么呢？恨未能生子？恨未做皇后？恨身边不是年轻的寿王而是淘虚了身子的老皇帝？恨老皇帝三次把她赶出宫去。总之，李白写杨玉环的无限恨，留给后人无限猜想。杨妃看了李白诗歌，非常喜欢。赞美她的文人成群结队，唯有李白说到她的心坎儿上了。《太真外传》载："杨妃笑领歌辞，意甚厚。"[1]

---

[1]《清平调词》三首合并赏析。

忆东山[1]（二首其一）

不向东山久，
蔷薇几度[2]花？
白云还自散，
明月落谁家？

[1] 东山：位于今浙江省绍兴市上虞区西南，传说是谢安曾游之处。
[2] 几度：几次。

　　谢安隐于东山三十年，携诸妓留佳话三百春；一出东山，指挥若定，横扫千军如席卷，八万人击败百万兵。李白对谢安是仰慕的，不恋权禄而又能为世所用，正是他自期、自比的对象。然而"翰林待诏"给他的却不过是皇帝随叫随到的文学侍从，何能"安黎元""济苍生"！隐，不甘心；仕，不如意。唯有浪迹纵酒以自昏秽。向往东山而又有负东山，白云明月正是诗人自比，"冠盖满京华"，奈何落谁家？

The Eastern Hill (I)

Once more I come to Eastern Hill.

How many times has blown the rose?

White clouds gather and scatter still.

Where sinks the moon of yore? Who knows?

乌栖曲

姑苏台①上乌栖时,
吴王②宫里醉西施。
吴歌楚舞欢未毕,
青山欲衔半边日。
银箭金壶③漏水多,
起看秋月坠江波,
东方渐高奈乐何!

①姑苏台:又名姑胥台,在苏州城外西南隅的姑苏山上。公元前505年,始建于吴王阖闾,后经夫差续建。极华丽,规模极宏大,耗资庞大,以供吴王夫差娱乐。
②吴王:吴王夫差。
③银箭金壶:指刻漏,古代计时工具。

  黄昏乌栖,吴歌楚舞未休,青山衔日,暗示时光悄然流逝。夜至,银箭金壶漏水,秋月坠江波,直至东方渐高,欢乐却不知休止。李白以姑苏台为背景,描绘吴王宫里醉生梦死之景。真可谓:花开花落不长久,落红满地归寂中。此诗巧用环境烘托,语言精准,韵律和谐,深刻讽刺了统治者的腐朽,让人在短短数语中感受到历史的沧桑与诗人的忧思,堪称佳作。

Crows Going Back to Their Nest
—Satire on the King of Wu

O'er Royal Terrace when crows flew back to their nest,
The king in Royal Palace feast'd his mistress drunk.
The Southern maidens sang and danced without a rest
Till beak-like mountain-peaks would peck the sun half sunk.
The golden clepsydra could not stop water's flow,
O'er river waves the autumn moon was hanging low.
But wouldn't the king enjoy his fill in Eastern glow?

下终南山①过②斛斯山人③宿置酒

暮从碧山下,
山月随人归。
却顾④所来径,
苍苍横翠微。
相携及田家,
童稚开荆扉⑤。
绿竹入幽径,
青萝拂行衣。
欢言得所憩,
美酒聊共挥⑥。
长歌吟松风⑦,
曲尽河星稀。
我醉君复乐,
陶然⑧共忘机⑨。

①终南山:秦岭。
②过:拜访。
③斛斯山人:一位复姓斛斯的隐士。
④却顾:回头望。
⑤荆扉:荆条编成的门。
⑥挥:举杯。
⑦松风:古乐府琴曲名,即《风入松曲》,此处也有歌声随风入林的意思。
⑧陶然:欢乐的样子。
⑨忘机:忘掉世俗的心机。

　　李白暮下终南山,山月相伴,回望翠微,意境空灵。至山人处,童稚开扉,绿竹幽径,青萝拂衣。相聚无隙,欢言共饮,长歌吟风,曲尽星稀。诗人沉醉其中,与友共乐忘机。好一幅主客尽欢、忘却世俗的田园美景图。此诗绘自然之美,

Descending Zhongnan Mountain and Meeting Husi the Hermit

At dusk I leave the hills behind,
The moon escorts me all the way.
Looking back, I see the path wind
Across the woods so green and grey.
We come to your cot hand in hand,
Your lad opens the gate for me.
Bamboos along the alley stand
And vines caress my cloak with glee.
I'm glad to talk and drink good wine
Together with my hermit friend.
We sing the songs of wind and pine,
And stars are set when singings end.
I'm drunk and you're merry and glad:
We both forget the world is sad.

抒闲适之情，语言优美，意境深远，让人感受着诗人的洒脱与自在。

月下独酌[1]（四首其一）

花间一壶酒，
独酌无相亲。
举杯邀明月，
对影成三人[2]。
月既不解饮，
影徒随我身。
暂伴月将[3]影，
行乐须及春[4]。
我歌月徘徊，
我舞影零乱。
醒时同交欢，
醉后各分散。
永结无情游，
相期[5]邈[6]云汉[7]。

[1] 独酌：一人饮酒。
[2] 三人：月亮、我、我的影子。
[3] 将：和。
[4] 及春：趁着青春年华。
[5] 相期：相约。
[6] 邈：遥远。
[7] 云汉：银河。

　　李白是充满浪漫主义色彩的诗人，这首诗就是其浪漫色彩呈现的经典之作。其于花间置一壶酒，却无人相随，孤独之感油然而生。然诗人并不消沉，笔锋一转，举杯邀月，对影成伴，化孤独为奇妙之境。诗人以月与影为伴，行乐于春景之中。歌时月徘徊，舞时影零乱，醒时同欢，醉后分散，

Drinking Alone under the Moon (I)

Amid the flowers, from a pot of wine

I drink alone beneath the bright moonshine.

I raise my cup to invite the Moon who blends

Her light with my Shadow and we're three friends.

The Moon does not know how to drink her share;

In vain my Shadow follows me here and there.

Together with them for the time I stay

And make merry before spring's spent away.

I sing and the Moon lingers to hear my song;

My Shadow's a mess while I dance along.

Sober, we three remain cheerful and gay;

Drunken, we part and each may go his way.

Our friendship will outshine all earthly love,

Next time we'll meet beyond the stars above.

尽显诗人的洒脱与豪放。最后,诗人渴望与月与影结下永世的情谊,相约在遥远的银河。整首诗情感跌宕起伏,既有孤独寂寞,又有自我排遣的洒脱,充分体现了李白豪放不羁的诗风与独特的人格魅力。

把酒问月

青天有月来几时?
我今停杯一问之。
人攀明月不可得,
月行却与人相随。
皎如飞镜临丹阙[1],
绿烟[2]灭尽清辉发。
但见宵从海上来,
宁知晓向云间没[3]?
白兔捣药秋复春,
嫦娥孤栖与谁邻?

①丹阙:朱红色的宫殿。
②绿烟:遮蔽月光的浓厚云雾。
③没(mò):淹没。

  咏月抒怀之作,李白堪称一流。本诗以奇崛之问"青天有月来几时?我今停杯一问之"开篇,尽显潇洒豪迈姿态。对着明月发出震撼人心的疑问,展现出诗人豁达奔放的心境和对宇宙奥秘的强烈好奇。人攀月不得,月却与人相随,充满了人们渴望得到那些看似完美、崇高的东西,却常常求而不得的哲理意味。明月如飞镜,清辉四溢,神秘莫测。进而

Reflections on the Moon While Drinking

When did the moon first come on high?

I stop drinking to ask the sky.

The moon's beyond the reach of man;

It follows us where'er it can.

Like mirror bright o'er palace wall,

When clouds disperse, it's seen by all.

At night, it rises out of the sea;

At dawn, who knows where it can be?

Jade Hare is not companion boon

For lonely Goddess of the Moon.

联想到白兔捣药、嫦娥孤栖,又添了神话色彩。"今人不见古时月,今月曾经照古人"一句,深刻地表达了时间的流转和人生的短暂,感慨万千。最后以"唯愿当歌对酒时,月光长照金樽里"作结,流露出对美好时光的珍惜和对生活的热爱之情。整首诗意境空灵,情感深沉,既有着对自然的赞美,又有着对人生的思考。

今人不见古时月,
今月曾经照古人。
古人今人若流水,
共看明月皆如此。
唯愿当歌对酒时,
月光长照金樽里。

We see the ancient moon no more,

But it has shone on men of yore.

Like flowing stream, they passed away;

They saw the moon as we do today.

I only wish when I drink wine,

Moonlight dissolve in goblet mine.

白云歌送刘十六①归山

楚山秦山皆白云,
白云处处长随君。
长随君,
君入楚山里,
云亦随君渡湘水②。
湘水上,
女萝衣,
白云堪卧君早归。

①刘十六:李白的朋友。
②湘水:湘江。

　　诗中写白云处处长随君,入楚山、渡湘水,一如诗人的牵挂。湘水上着松萝衣与白云相映,与自然相融,宁静和谐。"白云堪卧君早归",既表达出对友人归山的期盼,又流露出对自然的向往。全诗以白云为线索,将深情与自然之美融合,语言优美,充满浪漫色彩,尽显诗人对友人的祝福及对自由生活的憧憬。

Song of White Cloud
—Farewell Song to Liu the Recluse

From the mountains you come;to the mountains you go,

White clouds will follow you high and low, high and low.

When you come into Southern mountains high,

Following you, o'er Southern streams white clouds will fly.

O'er Southern water blue,

There's ivy cloak for you,

You should go back and lie on cloud as white clouds do.

辑四

我寄愁心与明月

秋日鲁郡尧祠亭上宴别杜补阙范侍御

我觉秋兴①逸,
谁云秋兴悲?
山将落日去,
水与晴空宜。
鲁酒白玉壶,
送行驻金羁②。
歇鞍憩古木,
解带挂横枝。
歌鼓③川上亭,
曲度神飙④吹。
云归碧海夕,
雁没青天时。
相失各万里,
茫然空尔⑤思。

①秋兴:因秋天而起兴致。
②驻金羁:停马。金羁,金制的马络头,这里代指马。
③歌鼓:唱歌打鼓。
④神飙:疾风。
⑤尔:指李白好友,即诗题里的杜补阙、范侍御。

此诗开篇李白就表明其观点:秋天带来的是一种超逸的兴致,而非传统意义上的悲秋之情。其以反问的语气,挑战世人普遍的悲秋观念,展现独特的审美体验和积极向上的人生态度,尽显豁达心境。山携落日,水映晴空,美景如画。鲁酒白玉壶,金羁送行,豪迈之情顿生。歇鞍古木,解带挂

Farewell to Two Friends in Lu on an Autumn Day

I feel that autumn's glad.

Who says that autumn's sad?

Hills bring down setting sun;

Water and sky seem one.

Drink wine from pot jade-white;

From golden horse alight.

Repose and set it free;

Hang belt upon old tree.

Chant by the stream aloud!

Songs soar into the cloud.

Back to blue sea clouds fly,

Wild geese lost in blue sky.

Like them well sever too,

In vain I'll long for you.

枝,随意自在。歌鼓川上亭,曲度似神飙,宴别场景热闹非凡。云归碧海,雁没青天,既壮美又暗示离别将至。末句"相失各万里,茫然空尔思",又流露出离别的惆怅与思念,让人感同身受。此诗情景交融,秋日之美与离别之情相得益彰,展现出李白独特的才情与情感深度。

鲁郡东石门[1]送杜二甫[2]

醉别复几日,
登临遍池台。
何时石门路,
重有金樽开?
秋波落泗水[3],
海色明徂徕[4]。
飞蓬各自远,
且尽手中杯。

[1]石门:山名,位于今山东省曲阜市东北。
[2]杜二甫:诗人杜甫。因排行第二,故称其为杜二甫。
[3]泗水:水名,位于今山东省东部。
[4]徂(cú)徕(lái):山名,在今山东泰安市东南。

  此诗以"醉别"开篇,又以"干杯"结束,既充满了李白式的豪放不羁和乐观开朗,又流露出他与杜甫之间的深厚情谊。诗中回忆醉别几日的欢乐,流露出对重逢的渴望。"秋波落泗水,海色明徂徕",秋景壮美,却因离别添上哀愁。又以飞蓬喻分别,洒脱中含不舍。此诗情感真挚,既有怀念与期待,又有惆怅与豪放,令人动容。

Farewell to Du Fu at Stone Gate

Before we part we've drunk for many days
And visit'd all the scenic spots and bays.
When at the Gate of Stone shall we meet and drain
Our brimming golden cups of wine again?
The autumn waves of River Si still flow;
The seaside mountains stand in morning glow.
You'll go away as thistle-down will fly,
So let us fill our cups and drink them dry.

沙丘①城下寄杜甫

我来竟何事?
高卧②沙丘城。
城边有古树,
日夕连秋声。
鲁酒不可醉,
齐歌空复情。
思君若汶水,
浩荡寄南征。

①沙丘:指唐代兖州治城瑕丘。
②高卧:高枕而卧,此处指闲居。

  李白和杜甫这两颗中国文学史上的璀璨明星,虽然年龄相差11岁,却结下了深厚的情谊,此诗便是一佐证。诗歌前半部分着重描写诗人在沙丘城的生活状态与周边环境。无聊闲居,迷茫孤独,为思念友人埋下伏笔。古树秋声,萧瑟凄清,诗人的孤寂之感透纸三分。后半部分情感喷薄而出。酒与歌无法慰藉其对杜甫的思念之情,唯将思念之情比作浩荡的汶水,日夜奔腾向南。这比喻既贴切又极具感染力,使整首诗的情感达到高潮。

To Du Fu from Sand Hill Town

Why have I come here after all

To live alone the whole day long ?

There're but old trees by city wall,

From dawn till dusk but Autumn's song.

I can't be soothed by wine of Lu,

Nor moved by local melody.

Like River Wen I think of you,

Whose waves roll southward endlessly.

戏赠杜甫

饭颗山①头逢杜甫,
头戴笠子②日卓午③。
借问④别来太瘦生⑤,
总为⑥从前作诗苦。

①饭颗山:山名,据传在长安一带。
②笠子:用竹箬或棕皮等编成的帽子。
③日卓午:指正午太阳当空。
④借问:请问。
⑤太瘦生:瘦弱。"生"是语气助词,唐时习语。
⑥总为:怕是为了。

《戏赠杜甫》充满诙谐意趣。诗中李白以轻松之语调侃杜甫拘束之态,似见两人的亲密无间。日正当中,不期而遇。头戴斗笠的子美呀,你为何如此清瘦?看似关心,却以调侃之语归因为作诗之苦,既体现出李白的洒脱不羁,又流露出其与杜甫的亲密关系。寥寥数语,勾勒出两位诗人的独特形象,让人在会心一笑中,感受他们真挚的情谊与别样的才情魅力。

Addressed Humorously to Du Fu

On top of Hill of Boiled Rice I met Du Fu,
Who in the noonday sun wore a hat of bamboo.
Pray, how could you have grown so thin since we did part?
Is it because the verse-composing wrung your heart?

梦游天姥①吟留别

海客谈瀛洲②,
烟涛微茫③信难求。
越人语天姥,
云霞明灭或可睹。
天姥连天向天横,
势拔五岳掩赤城。
天台一万八千丈,
对此欲倒东南倾。
我欲因之梦吴越,
一夜飞渡镜湖月。
湖月照我影,
送我至剡溪④。
谢公宿处今尚在,
渌⑤水荡漾清猿啼。

①天姥:天姥山,位于浙江省绍兴市新昌县以东。传说登山的人能听到神仙天姥的歌声,因此得名。
②瀛洲:古传说中的东海三座仙山之一(另两座是蓬莱和方壶)。
③微茫:模糊不清。
④剡(shàn)溪:水名,位于浙江省绍兴市嵊州市以南。
⑤渌(lù):清。

此诗犹如一幅奇幻画卷徐徐展开,景物繁多、场面热闹。李白入梦,畅游天姥山,那是一个神秘莫测的世界。云霞明灭,峰峦叠翠,仙人纷至沓来。熊咆龙吟、云雨天暗、电闪雷鸣、丘峦崩摧后,洞天石扉訇然中开,气势恢宏,震撼人心。诗人对梦幻世界大胆的想象和夸张的纵笔,正是对自由、

Mount Skyland Ascended in a Dream
—A Song of Farewell

Of fairy isles seafarers speak,

'Mid dimming mist and surging waves, so hard to seek;

Of Skyland Southerners are proud,

Perceivable through fleeting or dispersing cloud.

Mount Skyland threatens heaven, massed against the sky,

Surpassing the Five Peaks and dwarfing Mount Red Town.

Mount Heaven's Terrace, five hundred thousand feet high,

Nearby to the southeast, appears to crumble down.

Longing in dreams for Southern land, one night

I flew o'er Mirror Lake in moonlight.

My shadow's followed by moonbeams

Until I reach Shimmering Streams,

Where Hermitage of Master Xie can still be seen,

And clearly gibbons wail o'er rippling water green.

美好的向往和追求。可叹万事如流水，一去无返，梦醒时唯有万千感慨。"安能摧眉折腰事权贵，使我不得开心颜"，掷地有声、振聋发聩。此诗似一道璀璨流星，划过文学的天空，展现了诗人的豪迈不羁与对自由的执着追求，让我们在梦幻与现实的交织中，感受那无尽的诗意与力量。

脚著谢公⑥屐，
身登青云梯⑦。
半壁见海日，
空中闻天鸡⑧。
千岩万转路不定，
迷花倚石忽已暝⑨。
熊咆龙吟殷岩泉⑩，
栗深林兮惊层巅。
云青青⑪兮欲雨，
水澹澹⑫兮生烟。
列缺⑬霹雳，
丘峦崩摧。
洞天石扉，
訇然⑭中开。
青冥⑮浩荡不见底，
日月照耀金银台⑯。
霓为衣兮风为马，
云之君⑰兮纷纷而来下。

⑥谢公：指谢灵运。
⑦青云梯：指直穿云霄的山路。
⑧天鸡：神话传说中天上的鸡。每当太阳升起，天鸡一叫，天下的鸡都跟着它叫。
⑨暝：日落。
⑩殷岩泉：也即"岩泉殷"。殷，这里用作动词，震响。
⑪青青：黑森森的。
⑫澹澹：波浪起伏的样子。
⑬列缺：指闪电。
⑭訇（hōng）然：形容声音极大。
⑮青冥：指天空。
⑯金银台：金银建成的宫殿，指神仙的住所。
⑰云之君：云里的仙人。

I put Xie's pegged boot

Each on one foot,

And scale the mountain ladder to blue cloud.

On eastern cliff I see

Sunrise at sea,

And in mid-air I hear sky-cock crow loud.

The footpath meanders 'mid a thousand crags in the vale,

I'm lured by rocks and flowers when the day turns pale.

Bears roar and dragons howl and thunders the cascade,

Deep forests quake and ridges tremble, they're afraid!

From dark, dark cloud comes rain;

On pale, pale waves mists plane.

Oh! Lightning flashes

And thunder rumbles,

With stunning crashes

Peak on peak crumbles.

The stone gate of a fairy cavern under

Suddenly breaks asunder.

So blue, so deep, so vast appears an endless sky,

Where sun and moon shine on gold and silver terraces high.

Clad in the rainbow, riding on the wind,

The Lords of Clouds descend in a procession long.

虎鼓瑟兮鸾回车,
仙之人兮列如麻。
忽魂悸以魄动,
恍惊起而长嗟。
唯觉时之枕席,
失向来之烟霞。
世间行乐亦如此,
古来万事东流水。
别君去兮何时还?
且放白鹿[18]青崖间,
须行即骑访名山。
安能摧眉折腰事权贵,
使我不得开心颜!

[18]白鹿:传说中神仙多骑白鹿。

Their chariots drawn by phoenix disciplined,

And tigers playing for them a zither song,

Row upon row, like fields of hemp, immortals throng.

Suddenly my heart and soul stirred, I

Awake with a long, long sigh.

I find my head on pillow lie

And fair visions gone by.

Likewise all human joys will pass away

Just as east-flowing water of olden day.

I'll take my leave of you, not knowing for how long.

I'll tend a white deer among

The grassy slopes of the green hill

So that I may ride it to famous mountains at will.

How can I stoop and bow before the men in power

And so deny myself a happy hour?

登金陵凤凰台①

凤凰台上凤凰游,
凤去台空江自流。
吴宫②花草埋幽径,
晋代衣冠③成古丘。
三山④半落青天外,
二水⑤中分白鹭洲。
总为浮云⑥能蔽日,
长安⑦不见使人愁。

①凤凰台:在金陵凤凰山上。
②吴宫:三国时孙吴曾于金陵建都筑宫。
③衣冠:衣服帽子,此处代指豪门士族。
④三山:山名,位于金陵西南长江边。
⑤二水:指秦淮河流经南京后,西入长江,被白鹭洲截分为二支。
⑥浮云:喻奸佞之臣。
⑦长安:代指朝廷。

　　凤凰台空,江水流淌,尽显历史沧桑。吴宫花草、晋代衣冠皆成古丘,让人感慨时光易逝。"三山半落青天外,二水中分白鹭洲",诗人以宏大的视野,将三山与青天、二水与白鹭洲相结合,营造出一种开阔、悠远的意境,描绘出金陵(今南京)的壮丽景色。不仅展现了金陵的自然景观,也流露出

On Phoenix Terrace at Jinling

On Phoenix Terrace once phoenixes came to sing,
The birds are gone but still roll on the river's waves.
The ruined palace's buried 'neath the weeds in spring;
The ancient sages in caps and gowns all lie in graves.
The three-peak'd mountain is half lost in azure sky;
The two-fork'd stream by Egret Isle is kept apart.
As floating clouds can veil the bright sun from the eye,
Imperial Court now out of sight saddens my heart.

诗人对历史兴衰和人生沉浮的感慨。末句则表达了诗人对朝廷的忧虑和对长安的思念，将历史感慨与个人情思完美融合，意境深远，韵味无穷。

劳劳亭[1]

天下伤心处,
劳劳送客亭。
春风知[2]别苦,
不遣[3]柳条青。

[1]劳劳亭:位于今江苏省南京市西南,为古时送别之地。
[2]知:理解,懂得。
[3]遣:让。

　　李白因亭起意,借三国时期吴国所建的分别之所写人间别离。直言伤心别苦,又借春风有情,不让柳枝复青来催促离别。诗人的联想与奇想并发,感物抒情,联类不穷。悲莫悲兮生别离,自然之极,太白独步。

Pavilion Laolao

There is no place that oftener breaks the heart
Than the Pavilion seeing people part.
The wind of early spring knows parting grieves,
It will not green the roadside willow leaves.

丁都护歌[1]

云阳[2]上征去,
两岸饶商贾[3]。
吴牛[4]喘月时,
拖船一何苦!
水浊不可饮,
壶浆半成土。
一唱都护歌,
心摧泪如雨。
万人凿磐石,
无由达江浒[5]。
君看石芒砀[6],
掩泪悲千古!

①丁都护歌:乐府旧题。
②云阳:今江苏丹阳。
③饶商贾(gǔ):商人很多。
④吴牛:江淮间的水牛。
⑤江浒(hǔ):江边。
⑥石芒砀(dàng):石头又多又大。

李白自云阳(今江苏丹阳)乘船北上,两岸商贾云集、繁华热闹非凡的景象,没引起他的注意,偏偏是运河上的纤夫吸引了他的目光和笔力。酷热的盛夏、解渴的泥浆水、上征的太湖石、悲切的拉纤声,诗人借古曲《丁都护歌》写悲苦时事。生存的艰辛和两岸的富庶形成强烈反差,繁华背后的血泪辛酸,知者几人,痛者几人,珍惜者又有几人?

Song of the Tow-men

They tow a boat and upstream wade
Between two shores alive with trade.
Under the heat pants buffalo.
O think what pain it is to tow!
The water's muddy and can not
Be drunk: thick silt fills half the pot.
When tow-men sing their song's refrain,
With broken heart, tears fall like rain.
Ten thousand quarry-men would groan
To haul to riverside rough stone.
If rocky mountains could have ears,
Would they not melt into sad tears?

苏台①览②古

旧苑③荒台杨柳新,
菱歌④清唱不胜春。
只今惟有西江月,
曾照吴王宫里人⑤。

①苏台:指姑苏台,故址位于今江苏省苏州市西南姑苏山上。
②览:观览。
③旧苑:指苏台。
④菱歌:老百姓采菱时唱的民歌。
⑤吴王宫里人:指吴王夫差宫廷里的嫔妃。

The Ruin of the Gusu Palace

Deserted garden, crumbling terrace, willows green,
Sweet notes of Lotus Song cannot revive old spring.
All are gone but the moon o'er West River that's seen
The ladies fair who won the favor of the king.

越中①览古

越王勾践破吴归，
义士还家尽锦衣。
宫女如花满春殿，
只今惟有鹧鸪②飞。

①越中：指会稽，春秋时期越国的都城。旧址位于今浙江省绍兴市。
②鹧鸪：鸟名。

这两首诗是诗人游历江南的见闻，虽创作年份不同，但连起来品读更具意义。李白论及历史上吴王夫差、越王勾践盛衰荣败的转换，由目睹的废墟想到过去的繁华，曾经锦衣还乡的荣耀变成眼前的凄凉，"宫阙万千都做了土"。一句"只今惟有"说尽人事变化、兴废的无常。世间唯有变化本身才是不变的。如何在变化的世界中生存，看来不只是李白要寻找的答案，也是如今的我们探寻的方向。[1]

---

[1]《苏台览古》《越中览古》合并赏析。

The Ruin of the Capital of Yue

The king of Yue returned, having destroyed the foe,
His loyal men came home, with silken dress aglow,
His palace thronged with flower-like ladies fair;
Now we see but a frock of partridges flying there.

越女词（五首其一）

长干吴①儿女②，
眉目艳星月。
屐上足如霜，
不着鸦头袜③。

①吴：吴地，位于今长江下游江苏南部。
②儿女：指女儿。
③鸦头袜：指拇趾与其他四趾分开的袜子。

Songs of the Southern Lass (I)

The Southern lass is fair and bright,

Her eyes and brows shame moon and stars.

Her feet in sandals are frost-white,

The crow-head shoes would look like scars.

越女词（五首其三）

耶溪①采莲女，
见客棹歌②回。
笑入荷花去，
佯羞不出来。

①耶溪：若耶溪。
②棹歌：划船时唱的歌。

Songs of the Southern Lass (III)

A maiden gathers lotus in the creek,

Singing, she turns round, seeing passers-by.

Smiling, she hides 'mid lotus blooms her cheek

And won't appear again: she seems so shy.

越女词（五首其五）

镜湖水如月，
耶溪女如雪。
新妆荡新波，
光景①两奇绝。

①景：同"影"。

"三里不同音，五里不同俗"，低沸点的欣悦、好奇的兴奋激发诗人无尽感悟。写越女从群像写到个体，不细描容貌，一个"艳星月"就让人浮想联翩，少女的明媚直逼大脑。再则"不着鸦头袜"的赤足裸露出的肌肤细白如霜，让人沉醉。更何况越女的歌声、笑声，还有"欲说还羞"的情态，让初游江南的李白感到无比新奇。最后一首，更是把美景与美女相映衬，"奇绝"极尽赞叹。[1]

---

[1]《越女词》三首合并赏析。

Songs of the Southern Lass (V)

The waves of Mirror Lake look like moonbeams;
The maiden's dress like snow on waterside.
The rippling dress vies with the rippling stream,
We know not which by which is beautified.

渌水曲[1]

渌水明秋月,
南湖[2]采白蘋[3]。
荷花娇欲语,
愁杀[4]荡舟人。

[1] 渌水曲：古乐府曲名。
[2] 南湖：洞庭湖。
[3] 白蘋：一种水生植物。
[4] 愁杀：愁煞，愁到不能忍受之意。杀，置于动词后，表示极度。

　　这首五绝朴拙的用字，描绘出清新自然的月景。对美景的想象却被末句的"愁"字拉回。无心赏景，愁对月色，孤寂苦闷的诗人形象鲜明突出。人生不如意时，多少美景难通心曲。

Song of Green Water

O'er water green the autumn moon shines bright,
On Southern Lake they gather lilies white.
The lotus-blooms so lovely as to speak
Outshine the bashful oarswomen's fair cheek.

闻王昌龄①左迁②龙标③遥有此寄

杨花④落尽子规啼,
闻道龙标过五溪⑤。
我寄愁心与明月,
随风直到夜郎⑥西。

① 王昌龄:唐代诗人。
② 左迁:贬谪。
③ 龙标:地名,位于今贵州省锦屏县。古代常用任职之地的名字来称呼一个人。
④ 杨花:柳絮。
⑤ 五溪:武溪、巫溪、酉溪、沅溪、辰溪的总称,位于今湖南省西部。
⑥ 夜郎:唐代夜郎县,位于今湖南省怀化市沅陵县。

  身处扬州的李白听闻好友王昌龄被贬遥远的龙标,心中感愤,借杨花、子规起兴,即景生情,渲染凄凉哀愁的气氛。再托明月送慰藉,对诗友进行由衷的劝勉和宽慰。既有对其怀才不遇的惋惜,又饱含同情之意。《唐诗笺注》说"愁心"二句,何等缠绵悱恻!而"我寄愁心",犹觉比"隔千里兮共明月"意更深挚。

To Wang Changling Banished to the West

All willow-down has fallen and sad cuckoos cry

To hear you banished southwestward beyond Five Streams.

I would confide my sorrow to the moon on high

For it will follow you west of the Land of Dreams.

战城南[1]

去年战,
桑干源[2];
今年战,
葱河[3]道。
洗兵[4]条支[5]海上波,
放马天山雪中草。
万里长征战,
三军尽衰老。
匈奴以杀戮为耕作,
古来惟见白骨黄沙田。

[1]战城南:乐府古题。
[2]桑干源:桑干河,为今永定河之上游。
[3]葱河:葱岭河。今有南北两段。南为叶尔羌河,北为喀什噶尔河,都在新疆西南。
[4]洗兵:表示胜利结束战争。传说周武王出师遇雨,认为是老天洗刷兵器,后擒纣灭商,后代遂以"洗兵"表示胜利结束战争。
[5]条支:汉西域古国名。在今伊拉克底格里斯河、幼发拉底河之间。此泛指西域。

  战无休,民生艰! 天宝年间,唐玄宗轻动干戈,逞威边远,却几经失败。"去年"战北方,"今年"打西方,东征西讨,转旆不息。海上洗兵器,天山牧战马,频繁征战,战场广远。将士的青春、精力在无谓的战争中耗尽。历史的教训还不够吗? 匈奴人好杀戮,他们的田野中只见白骨埋黄沙。秦筑长城防胡人,汉时烽烟仍高举,不休! 穷兵黩武,争斗不息。

Fighting South of the Town

Last year we fought

At River's source;

This year we fight

Along its course.

We've washed our swords in Parthian seas oft bloody stains,

And grazed our horses on the grass in mountain's snow.

For miles and miles we made campaigns

Till weak and old our warriors grow.

The Tartars live on killing as on ploughing land,

Bleach'd bones of olden times are buried in the sand.

战争残酷，古来征战几人回，徒剩战马悲鸣思主；战场凄凉，乌鸦啄死人肠，飞起挂树梢。士兵的鲜血染红野草，将军们也空无所获。可叹：兴，百姓苦；亡，百姓苦！《六韬》说："圣人号兵为凶器，不得已而用之。"全诗以此语意作结，点明主题。一桩桩惨烈的战事，一宗宗严酷的史实，积聚到诗人胸中，沉思、悲愤直诉笔端。叙议结合，长短相间，全是诗人喷涌出的忧国悯民之情。陈古刺今，此乐府之至显者。

秦家筑城⑥备胡处,
汉家还有烽火燃。
烽火燃不息,
征战无已时。
野战格斗死,
败马号鸣向天悲。
乌鸢⑦啄人肠,
衔飞上挂枯树枝。
士卒涂草莽,
将军空尔为⑧。
乃知兵者是凶器,
圣人不得已而用之。

⑥秦家筑城:指秦始皇筑长城以防匈奴。
⑦鸢(yuān):老鹰。
⑧空尔为:一无所获。

Under the Qin against the foe Great Wall was raised;
Under the Han the beacon fires still blazed.
See beacon fires on the frontier!
Till warriors fight from year to year.
In wilderness the fighters die,
Riderless horses neigh toward the sky;
Crows pecking human entrails flee
And hang them on a withered tree.
The blood of soldiers smears the grass.
Without them what could generals do?
War is a fearful thing, alas!
For rulers wise, 'twould be the last means resorted to.

辑五

举杯消愁愁更愁

听蜀僧濬①弹琴

蜀僧抱绿绮②,
西下峨眉峰。
为我一挥手,
如听万壑松③。
客心洗流水④,
余响入霜钟。
不觉碧山暮,
秋云暗几重?

①蜀僧濬:蜀地名为濬的僧人。
②绿绮:琴名。
③万壑松:万壑松声,此处指琴声。
④流水:一语双关,既指僧濬的琴声,也暗用了伯牙善弹的典故。

听琴,听由峨眉山下来的和尚濬弹琴,家乡人出场必须气派!抱着名为绿绮的名琴,潇洒一挥手,就如万千山谷中的松涛声,铿锵辽远,涤荡人心。"伯牙挥手,钟期听声",诗人感慨,高山流水遇知音。通过音乐的媒介建立的知音之感成为这首五律的主要发力点。琴声洗心,余音不绝,入神聆听,不知日暮将至。此诗明快畅晓,不着用力痕迹,"清水出芙蓉,天然去雕饰"。

On Hearing a Monk from Shu Playing His Lute

A monk from Shu his green lute brings,

Coming down the west peak of Mount Brow.

He sweeps his fingers o'er its strings,

I hear the wind through pine-trees sough.

A running stream washes my heart,

With evening bells its echo's loud.

I do not feel the sun depart

From mountains green and autumn cloud.

寄东鲁二稚子

吴地桑叶绿,
吴蚕已三眠。
我家寄东鲁,
谁种龟阴田①?
春事②已不及,
江行复茫然。
南风吹归心,
飞堕酒楼前。
楼东一株桃,
枝叶拂青烟。
此树我所种,
别来向三年。

①龟阴田:指李白在山东的田地。
②春事:春天耕种之事。

此诗一扫李白诗歌惯有的浪漫和豪放,尽显柔情与思念。诗从吴地桑叶绿、吴蚕三眠起笔,牵出对东鲁家园的牵挂,谁种龟阴田的疑问饱含对家的担忧。归心被南风吹起,飞堕酒楼前,那楼东边的桃树见证时光流逝。娇女平阳折花倚桃边,泪流满面;小儿伯禽与姐齐肩,相偎桃树下无人怜爱——

Written for My Two Children in East Lu

Mulberry leaves in Southern land are green,

The silkworms thrice in sleep must have been.

In Eastern Lu my family stay still.

Who'd help to sow our fields north of Lu Hill?

It's now too late to do farmwork of spring.

What then am I to do while travelling?

The southern wind is blowing without stop,

My heart flies back to my old familiar wine shop.

East of the shop there's a peach tree I've missed,

Its branches must be waving in bluish mist.

It is the tree I plant'd three years ago,

细节的想象展现诗人柔情。念及此,内心煎熬而焦灼,竟使李白失去常态模样,撕下白绢写下心中思念,其情如汶阳川水般深沉浩荡,令人动容。

桃今与楼齐,
我行尚未旋。
娇女字平阳,
折花倚桃边。
折花不见我,
泪下如流泉。
小儿名伯禽,
与姐亦齐肩。
双行桃树下,
抚背复谁怜?
念此失次第③,
肝肠日忧煎。
裂素④写远意,
因之汶阳川。

③失次第:情绪不定。
④裂素:裁剪白绢以绘画作文。素,白绢。

If it has grown to reach the roof, I don't know.
I have not been at home for three long years.
I can imagine my daughter appears
Beside the tree and plucks a flower pink.
Without seeing me, she must have, I think,
Shed copious tears. My younger son has grown
Up to his sister's shoulders. 'Neath full-blown.
Peach tree they stand side by side. But who's there
To pat them on the back? I feel, whene'er
I think of this, so painful that I write
And send to them this poem on silk white.

秦王扫六合

秦王扫六合,
虎视何雄哉!
挥剑决浮云,
诸侯尽西来。
雄图发英断,
大略驾群才。
收兵铸金人,
函谷正东开。
铭功会稽岭,
骋望琅玡台。
刑徒七十万,
起土骊山隈①。

① 隈:山水弯曲的地方。

此诗全面评价了秦始皇的功过。前半部分颂扬秦始皇之雄才大略和统一业绩;后半部分根据历史事实进行生动艺术描写,讽刺了秦王骄奢淫逸及妄想长生的荒唐行为。咏史,却不仅仅为秦始皇而发。唐玄宗和秦始皇颇相类似:两人都曾励精图治,而后来又变得骄奢无度,最后迷信方士妄求长生,

The Emperor of Qin

The Emperor had swept the world of his foes,

Looking around like a tiger he rose.

He broke the floating clouds while wielding swords,

Westward to pay their homage came all lords.

He made great plans and formed decisions wise,

In front of him all heroes dwarfed in size.

He melted weapons into statues of brass,

And opened to the East the frontier pass.

He built a monument on Eastern Hill,

And rode to Southern Tower to gaze his fill.

He worked seven hundred thousand slaves

To build in deep mountain recess his graves.

结果必然是贻害于国家。全诗史实与夸张、想象结合，叙事与议论、抒情结合，欲抑先扬，跌宕生姿，既有批判现实精神，又有浪漫奔放激情，是李白古风中的力作。

尚采不死药,
茫然使心哀。
连弩射海鱼,
长鲸正崔嵬②。
额鼻象五岳,
扬波喷云雷。
鬐鬣③蔽青天,
何由睹蓬莱?
徐市载秦女,
楼船几时回?
但见三泉下,
金棺葬寒灰!

②崔嵬:高大的样子。
③鬐(qí)鬣(liè):鱼、龙的脊鳍。

He sought elixir of immortality,

These contradictory deeds puzzle me.

He bent his bow to shoot the monster whale

Sweeping the sea with its enormous tail.

Its head and nose erect'd like mountains proud,

And water spout'd like thunder and like cloud.

Its dorsal fin might cover azure sky.

Could seamen find the Fairy Islands high?

The alchemist with maidens went to sea.

When could their galleys come back? We but see

Buried in underworld, the ashes cold

Of Emperor of Qin in coffin made of gold!

登高丘而望远海

登高丘,
望远海。
六鳌①骨已霜,
三山流安在?
扶桑②半摧折,
白日沉光彩。
银台金阙如梦中,
秦皇汉武空相待。
精卫费木石,
鼋鼍③无所凭。
君不见,
骊山茂陵尽灰灭,
牧羊之子来攀登!

①六鳌:神话中负载五座仙山的六只大龟。
②扶桑:神话中的树木名。
③鼋(yuán)鼍(tuó):神话传说中的巨鳖和猪婆龙(鳄鱼)。

登高望远,不写所见之景,反倒写高山大海的神话传说。六鳌成枯骨,三山已经是过眼云烟。扶桑摧折,太阳的光彩沉没殆尽。"银台金阙"犹如梦中烟云,秦皇汉武寻求的长生药亦如幻影。精卫填海,徒劳无功;鼋鼍为梁,不足为凭。神话传说就是虚妄。妄想长生的秦始皇、汉武帝穷兵黩武一

Mounting a Height and Viewing the Sea

Mounting a height,

I gaze afar.

Six Giant Turtles' bones emerge on sea, frost-white,

I do not see where the Three Fairy Mountains are.

The Tree Divine half broken,

The sun's great splendours wane.

Celestial palace is a dream unwoken

Emperors sought in vain.

The sea could not be filled with stones,

Nor could the gap by Turtles' bones.

Have we not seen imperial tombs in ruins lie,

Which shepherds set on fire?

世,换来的也不过是宫殿陵墓都倾废荒芜。他们也终归一死,风光不再。诗人托名讽刺秦始皇、汉武帝迷信求仙、穷兵黩武,实则嘲笑天宝十年(751)已沉溺佛道,奢求长生、荒淫误国的唐玄宗。感时伤世,抨古讽今,此时诗人虽落泊飘零,但仍心系朝廷,心系国运。

盗贼劫宝玉,
精灵竟何能?
穷兵黩武今如此,
鼎湖飞龙安可乘?

The bandits came to rob your jewels of value high.

What could you do, imperial lier?

Such is the end you warmongers obtained.

Could immortality be ever gained?

北风行

烛龙①栖寒门,
光耀犹旦开。
日月照之何不及此?
惟有北风号怒天上来。
燕山雪花大如席,
片片吹落轩辕台。
幽州思妇十二月,
停歌罢笑双蛾摧②。
倚门望行人,
念君长城③苦寒良④可哀。
别时提剑救边去,
遗此虎文金鞞靫⑤。

①烛龙:古代神话传说中的龙。人面龙身而无足,居住在极北极寒之地,睁眼为昼,闭眼为夜。
②双蛾摧:双眉紧锁,形容悲伤的样子。双蛾,女子的双眉。
③长城:古诗中常以此泛指北方前线。
④良:实在。
⑤鞞(bǐng)靫(chá):盛箭器。

此诗通过描写一个北方妇女对丈夫战死的悲愤心情,揭露和抨击了安禄山在北方挑起战争的罪行。诗人从一个"伤北风雨雪,行人不归"的题材,开掘出控诉战争罪恶、同情人民痛苦的主题,从而赋予了作品深刻的思想意义。诗人善用一连串动作来刻画人物的内心世界,"停歌""罢笑""双蛾

The North Wind

The candle-holding Dragon curls o'er Polar Gate,

Only at dawn his flickering light will radiate.

Nor sun nor moon will shine there far and nigh,

Only the howling northern wind blows down from the sky.

The snowflakes from north mountains, big as pillows white,

Fall flake on flake upon Yellow Emperor's Height.

The twelfth moon sees the wife in lonely bower sit,

She will nor sing nor smile, with eyebrows tightly knit.

She leans against the door and looks at passers-by,

Thinking of her husband who with cold might shiver

Beyond the Great wall and sigh.

When he started, his sword in hand,

To save the borderland.

He left her two white-feathered arrows in a golden quiver.

摧""倚门望"等细节塑造了一个忧心忡忡、愁肠百结的思妇形象。结尾北风怒号、飞雪漫天，满目凄凉的景象，反衬出思妇愁恨的深广和她悲愤不能自已的强烈感情，有着震撼人心的力量。

中有一双白羽箭,
蜘蛛结网生尘埃。
箭空在,
人今战死不复回。
不忍见此物,
焚之已成灰。
黄河捧土尚可塞,
北风雨雪恨难裁!

The pair of arrows 'mid cobwebs and dust remain.
Her lord who fell in battle won't come back again.
How could she bear to see the tiger-striped quiver?
She tries to burn it into ashes.
Building a dam, we may stop the flow of Yellow River.
How could the northern wind assuage her grief that gashes!

横江[1]词（六首其一）

人道横江好，
侬道[2]横江恶。
一风三日[3]吹倒山，
白浪高于瓦官阁[4]。

[1] 横江：横江浦，古长江渡口。在今安徽省马鞍山市和县东南，位于长江西北岸。
[2] 道：一作"言"。
[3] 三日：一作"一月"。
[4] 瓦官阁：寺阁名。

　　开笔借用口语中的"人道""侬道"，地方色彩和生活气息浓烈。"横江好""横江恶"，一扬一抑，直率表达情感。也许诗人急欲赶路，却被狂风猛浪阻在天门山。巨浪滔滔，排山倒海般奔袭过来，那白浪似比瓦官阁还高。极尽夸张，把北上的急切和受阻的焦虑融为一体。李白借景而发，感受真切。有限畅通的道路产生了多少生活的蕴味，如今一味图快的时代不复理解。

The Crosswise River (I)

They say the Crosswise River good;
I say the Crosswise River rude.
If winds should blow three days,
E'en hills would be blown down,
And waves rise higher than the Temple in the town.

山中问答

问余^①何意栖碧山,
笑而不答心自闲。
桃花流水窅然^②去,
别有天地非人间。

①余:我,指诗人自己。
②窅(yǎo)然:深邈遥远的样子。

    李白曾多次隐居山林。出川以后,从唐玄宗开元十五年(727)开始,在湖北安陆居住十年,曾隐居白兆山桃花岩。这首诗便抒发了他隐居生活自在天然的情趣,也体现了其矛盾心理。李白的隐居不是遁世,而是想等待时机到来,做一番济苍生、安社稷的事业。此诗在风格上有一种寓庄于谐的味道,愤世嫉俗与乐观浪漫奇妙地统一在了他的作品中,体现出矛盾的对立统一。

A Dialogue in the Mountain

I dwell among green hills and someone asks me why,

My mind carefree, I smile and give him no reply.

Peach blossoms fallen on running water pass by,

This is an earthly paradise beneath the sky.

自遣

对酒不觉暝^①,
落花盈我衣。
醉起步^②溪月,
鸟还人亦稀。

①暝：黄昏。
②步：散步。

　　自遣，自我消遣，仅从题目就知诗人李白心情不佳。为何？不知。只知诗人对酒。与谁对呢？落花、溪月还是自己的影子？喝多了，喝醉了，喝到鸟归巢人稀少，孤独寂寞，独自惆怅。

Solitude

I'm drunk with wine
And with moonshine,
With flowers fallen o'er the ground
And o'er me the blue-gowned.
Sobered, I stroll along the stream
Whose ripples gleam,
I see not a bird
And hear not a word.

独坐敬亭山①

众鸟高飞尽,
孤云独去闲②。
相看两不厌,
只有敬亭山。

①敬亭山：在今安徽省宣城市北。
②闲：形容云飘来飘去,悠然自得的样子。

　　鸟尽、云去,天空澄澈宁静,渺无一物,唯有敬亭山,对看良久而不厌弃。诗人只写景,情在景外。读来只见诗人寂然独坐,观众鸟高飞、孤云飘移,不料连众鸟与孤云都离他而去！下半部分忽然旁枝逸出,道是青山相对,含情脉脉,令人莞尔。然而紧接着心绪一荡：世间万物,唯青山不厌,这是何等孤独！再一转念：生命逆旅本无依,浮世三千有此一山,足矣！

　　佛曰"众生平等",庄子曰"齐物我",山与人,差相似！相看两不厌,李白真赤子之魂、潇洒之人也！

Sitting Alone in Face of Peak Jingting

All birds have flown away, so high;
A lonely cloud drifts on, so free.
We are not tired, the Peak and I,
Nor I of him, nor he of me.

宣州谢朓楼饯别校书叔云

弃我去者,
昨日之日不可留;
乱我心者,
今日之日多烦忧。
长风万里送秋雁,
对此可以酣①高楼。
蓬莱文章建安骨②,
中间小谢③又清发④。
俱怀逸兴壮思飞,
欲上青天揽明月。
抽刀断水水更流,
举杯消愁愁更愁。
人生在世不称意,
明朝散发⑤弄扁舟⑥。

①酣:畅饮。
②建安骨:建安风骨,指建安时期的文学风格。
③小谢:指谢朓,字玄晖,南朝齐诗人。后人将他和谢灵运并称为小谢、大谢。这里作者用以自喻。
④清发:指清新的诗文风格。
⑤散发:不束冠,即不入仕途。
⑥弄扁舟:乘小舟归隐江湖。

开篇似汹涌波涛,直抒诗人心中郁结。高楼之上,长风万里送秋雁,壮阔之景与内心烦忧相映。此时的诗人在谢朓楼饯别,壮志难酬与离情别绪交织。愁苦缠身,无力摆脱,既不称意,那就披散头发,独上扁舟,纵意江湖……无奈与

Farewell to Uncle Yun, the Imperial Librarian, at Xie Tiao's Pavilion in Xuanzhou

What left me yesterday

Can be retained no more;

What troubles me today

Are the times for which I feel sore.

In autumn wind for miles and miles the wild geese fly.

Let's drink, in face of this, in the pavilion high.

Your writing's forcible like ancient poets while

Mine is in Junior Xie's clear and spirited style.

Both of us have an ideal high:

We would reach the moon in the sky.

Cut running water with a sword, 'twill faster flow;

Drink wine to drown your sorrow, it will heavier grow.

If we despair of all human affairs,

Let us roam in a boat with loosened hairs!

逃避，洒脱与不羁，都在这首诗中交汇。看似李白为李云饯行而作，但更多的是抒发他自己怀才不遇、壮志难酬的愤懑，以及对现实的不满和对自由的向往。整首诗情感跌宕起伏，在豪放与惆怅间交织，尽显诗人的才情与胸怀。

秋登宣城谢朓北楼[①]

江城[②]如画里,
山晚望晴空。
两水[③]夹明镜,
双桥落彩虹[④]。
人烟寒橘柚,
秋色老梧桐。
谁念北楼上,
临风怀谢公[⑤]?

①谢朓北楼:南齐诗人谢朓任宣城太守时所建。
②江城:指宣城。
③两水:宛溪、句溪。
④彩虹:指桥在水中的倒影。
⑤谢公:谢朓。

　　天宝十三载(754),李白从金陵再度来到宣城,登上谢朓北楼。眼见"江城如画里":晴空万里,溪水如镜,桥身似虹,秋野炊烟处,橘柚深碧,梧桐微微黄。景色如故,人却无踪。当年的谢朓还有谁记得,现在就只有和你一样受排挤、不得志的我想着你,凭借山水寻求慰藉。

On Ascending the North Tower One Autumn Day

The scroll-like River-town's steeped in twilight,
In view of mountains 'neath a lucid sky.
Two rivers, mingling, form a mirror bright;
Two bridges like rainbows fallen from on high.
The cottage smoke has chilled the orange flower;
The autumn hue has oldened parasol trees.
Who ever dreamed I'd come up Northern Tower
To meditate on Xie in western breeze?

送友人

青山横北郭①,
白水绕东城。
此地一为别,
孤蓬②万里征。
浮云游子意,
落日故人情。
挥手自兹③去,
萧萧④班马⑤鸣。

①郭:在城墙外围加筑的一道城墙。
②蓬:一种植物,干枯后遇风即飞。此处比喻远行的朋友。
③兹:这里。
④萧萧:马的嘶鸣声。
⑤班马:离群的马。

  山环水绕的城外,故人相别,游子似孤蓬,万里无故人。浮云落日都不忍离去,久久地盘桓,挥手相别,人影渐远,唯听见萧萧的马鸣。离愁深情婉转,忧思深彻真挚。然青山、白水、浮云、落日又将这婉转之情转调成辽远疏阔的大境界;色调的明朗又将这忧思转调成壮伟之行,意味深远却又洒脱自然。

Farewell to a Friend

Green mountains bar the northern sky;
White water girds the eastern town.
Here is the place to say goodbye,
You'll drift out, lonely thistledown.
Like floating cloud you'll float away;
With parting day I'll part from you.
We wave and you start on your way,
Your horse still neighs: "Adieu! Adieu!"

秋浦①歌（十七首其十四）

炉火②照天地，
红星乱紫烟。
赧郎③明月夜，
歌曲动寒川。

①秋浦：地名，在今安徽贵池西。
②炉火：唐代，秋浦盛产铜，此处指炼铜的炉火。
③赧（nǎn）郎：被炉火映得脸红的炼铜工匠。

　　炉火熊熊照天地，火花四溅紫烟起。热火朝天的冶炼场景让李白感到新奇、兴奋，不由得惊叹。明月高悬夜不寐，冶炼工人脸通红。不知疲倦汗珠落，高歌一曲河水动。此诗讴歌健美强壮、勤劳乐观、充满活力的工人，生机盎然。秋浦是唐代银、铜的产地之一，而表现冶炼工人的诗极少。

Songs of Autumn Pool (XIV)

The furnace fire makes bright the earth and sky,
Into the purple smoke red sparks wild fly.
The blacksmiths' faces flush in moonlit night,
Their songs would fill the river cold with fright.

秋浦歌（十七首其十五）

白发三千丈，
缘①愁似个②长。
不知明镜里，
何处得秋霜③？

① 缘：因为。
② 个：这样，这般。
③ 秋霜：指白发。

"愁"，道出李白在此诗中的情感。五十多岁的他看见镜中已生白发的自己，悲从心来。当年"奋其志能，愿为辅弼"的抱负只换来三千丈的白发。老去已成定局，不甘的是所志不遂。李白极尽夸张道说心中悲愤。奇意奇调，真千古一人。

Songs of Autumn Pool（XV）

My whitened hair would make a long, long cord,

As long as I am often bored.

I know not how the mirror bright

Reflects a head with hoarfrost white.

赠汪伦[1]

李白乘舟将欲行,
忽闻岸上踏歌[2]声。
桃花潭[3]水深千尺,
不及汪伦送我情。

[1]汪伦：李白的朋友。
[2]踏歌：一边唱歌，一边用脚踏地打着节拍。
[3]桃花潭：水潭名，在今安徽省泾县西南。

　　古今送别诗，以此首最直白、最洒脱、最性情、最浅显，也最为人熟知！"深千尺"，用极度的夸张，将潭水的深度进行了不切实际的夸大描述，强烈地表现出李白对汪伦送行情谊的感受之深。在诗人心中，汪伦的情谊比千尺深潭还要深沉。读者能够直观地感受到两人之间友情的深厚程度，产生深刻的印象。呼应"不及汪伦送我情"，使整首诗的意境更加深远，也让这份真挚的友情穿越千年，熠熠生辉。

To Wang Lun Who Comes to Bid Me Farewell

I, Li Bai sit aboard a ship about to go,

When suddenly on shore footsteps and songs o'erflow.

The Lake of Peach Blossom is a thousand fathoms deep,

But not so deep as the friendship Wang Lun and I keep.

哭晁卿衡[1]

日本晁卿辞帝都[2],
征帆一片绕蓬壶[3]。
明月[4]不归沉碧海[5],
白云愁色满苍梧。

①晁卿衡：指晁衡，日本人，原名阿倍仲麻吕。唐开元五年（717）来中国求学，后改名为朝衡。朝通"晁"。卿，尊称。
②帝都：指长安。
③蓬壶：蓬莱、方壶，都是传说中的仙山。
④明月：指品德高洁如明月的人士，此处指晁衡。
⑤沉碧海：指溺亡在海中。

晁衡，原名阿倍仲麻吕，是李白结识的日本友人。753—754年间，晁衡辞别生活和为官多年的长安，乘船回家乡日本，在海上遇风浪失联，却被误传已亡。李白闻讯，悲痛不已，写下此诗悼念：如明月沉碧海，高洁有才的晁衡不幸遇难，天宇都悲恸,显得愁容满面。李白用丰富的想象借景抒情，把失去友人的悲痛用文字传达出来。

Elegy on Abe Nakamaro

My Japanese friend Abe left the imperial shore,

His single sail turned round for the three Fairy Isles.

The moon has sunk in the sea to return no more,

The land's o'erspread with gloomy clouds for miles and miles.

永王东巡歌（十一首其二）

三川①北虏②乱如麻，
四海南奔③似永嘉④。
但用东山谢安石⑤，
为君谈笑静胡沙⑥。

①三川：指洛阳，因其有河、洛、伊三川，故名。
②北虏：指安禄山叛军。
③南奔：指难民南奔避难。
④永嘉：永嘉之乱。西晋怀帝永嘉五年（311），匈奴军队在刘渊之子刘聪率领下，击败西晋京师洛阳的守军，攻陷洛阳并大肆抢掠杀戮，俘虏晋怀帝等王公大臣。
⑤谢安石：谢安，字安石，东晋名士。
⑥胡沙：指叛军。

　　天宝十五年（756），安禄山起兵造反攻陷潼关后，唐玄宗仓皇出逃，命其子永王李璘经营长江流域。身在庐山的李白被永王三请召为僚佐，随军途中写下十一首《永王东巡歌》，此为第二首。叛军"乱如麻"，多且凶，百姓如在水深火热中，像极晋代永嘉之乱，北方胡人造天下大难。国灾民难，爱憎

Song of Eastern Expedition of Prince Yong (II)

Three River Valleys overrun by Northern foes,
People within four seas flee to the Southern land.
If Master Xie again from Eastern Mountain rose,
He'd quell with ease the rebels as he'd sprinkle sand.

分明。诗人自比淝水大败敌军的谢安,同是东山再起,却不减当年雄心。辅佐王师的豪迈、乐观之情尽在"静胡沙"的谈笑间。成竹在胸、指挥若定,欲"挽狂澜于既倒"。诗人的爱国热情得到充分体现。

与史郎中钦听黄鹤楼上吹笛

一为迁客[①]去长沙,
西望长安不见家。
黄鹤楼中吹玉笛,
江城[②]五月落梅花[③]。

①迁客:被贬之人。
②江城:指江夏,今湖北武汉武昌。
③落梅花:古曲名。

"黄鹤一去不复返,白云千载空悠悠。"年逾花甲、功名蹭蹬的李白再次登上黄鹤楼。流放夜郎,长安无望,以贾谊贬长沙入典有愤懑也有辩白,然而前途茫茫,终是悲凉。偏那楼中笛音竟是《梅花落》,凄清怅惘凌然生寒,似见皑皑冰雪漫天落红——落的分明是胸中泪心中血啊!"仰天大笑出门去,我辈岂是蓬蒿人"就是个笑话!眼前景,耳中乐,而有弦外之音,更显凄怆。

On Hearing the Flute in Yellow Crane Tower

Since I was banished to the riverside town,
Looking westward, I've found no house I'd call my own.
Hearing in Yellow Crane Tower the flute's sad tune,
I seem to see mume blossoms fall in the fifth moon.

辑六

轻舟已过万重山

早发[1]白帝城

朝辞[2]白帝彩云间,
千里江陵[3]一日还。
两岸猿声啼不住[4],
轻舟已过万重山。

①发:出发,启程。
②辞:辞别,告别。
③江陵:今湖北省荆州市。
④住:停止。

    李白是五、七言绝句的圣手。其七绝韵味醇美,音节和谐流畅,感情真率,语言生动。这首脍炙人口的诗歌便是其七绝代表作之一。李白因永王李璘案被流放夜郎,行至白帝城的时候,忽然收到赦免的消息,惊喜交加,随即乘舟返回江陵。诗歌描摹了白帝城至江陵一段长江水急流速、舟行若飞的情况,把遇赦后如出笼的鸟一样的兴奋心情和江山的壮丽多姿、顺水行舟的流畅轻快融为了一体。全诗如有神助,不假雕琢,浑然天成。

Leaving the White Emperor Town for Jiangling

Leaving at dawn the White Emperor crowned with cloud,

I've sailed a thousand li through Canyons in a day.

With monkeys' sad adieux the riverbanks are loud;

My skiff has left ten thousand mountains far away.

与夏十二①登岳阳楼

楼观岳阳尽,
川迥②洞庭开。
雁引愁心去,
山衔好月来。
云间连下榻,
天上接行杯③。
醉后凉风起,
吹人舞袖回。

①夏十二:李白的朋友,排行十二,故名。
②迥:远。
③行杯:传杯饮酒。

　　流放夜郎被赦,那个诗酒李白似乎回魂了,阔达飘逸翩然而至。一"尽"一"迥"一"开",视线之辽远与岳阳楼之高尽出;一"引"一"衔"赋雁、山以情,愁心去、好月来,正是景语乃情语,痛快!好酒连杯,置身高楼若云间下榻、天上畅饮,美哉!归去尚舞袖翩翩,何等舒展惬意,直把自己当仙人了。全篇融写景、叙事、抒情于一体,自然浑成,不言楼高而读者了然,是谓"堂上言"。

*Ascending the Tower of Yueyang
with Xia the Twelfth*

On scenes so vast the Tower feasts our eye;

The river stretches into the Lake of South.

Taking away our sorrow, wild geese fly;

Green mountains throw the moon up from their mouth.

Make of white cloud a comfortable bed,

And pass around wine cups in azure skies.

Drunken, let cooling breezes blow and spread

Our dancing sleeves which flap like butterflies.

陪族叔刑部侍郎晔及中书贾舍人至游洞庭（五首其二）

南湖秋水夜无烟，
耐可①乘流直上天？
且就洞庭赊②月色，
将船买酒白云边。

① 耐可：怎可。
② 赊：欠。

759年，李晔、贾至和李白分别被贬，前往贬地时于洞庭湖相遇并结伴游玩。洞庭湖又称南湖，起句用干净的白描，写出清秋夜月照湖，湖面宽广澄澈，激起谪仙人羽化遗世的联想：上青天去。耐可，怎么上呢？算了，不纠结。凡间月色太美，暂且留下，拿月光去白云边赊酒寻欢吧。"赊月色"想象奇特大胆，引人遐思。在他的《送韩侍御之广德》中也出现过"暂就东山赊月色，酣歌一夜送泉明"。自然美景，人所共适。李白在清风明月中忘怀得失之患，随遇而安、旷达洒脱之情倾泄而出。

On Lake Dongting (II)

Vaporless is the Southern Lake on autumn night.
Could we be borne to Heaven by the rising tide?
If we could borrow from Lake Dongting the moonlight
To guide us skyward, we'd drink with clouds by our side.

江上吟

木兰之枻①沙棠舟,
玉箫金管②坐两头。
美酒樽中置千斛,
载妓随波任去留。
仙人有待乘黄鹤,
海客无心随白鸥。
屈平③词赋悬日月,
楚王台榭空山丘。
兴酣落笔摇五岳,
诗成笑傲凌沧洲。
功名富贵若长在,
汉水亦应西北流。

①枻:同"楫",即船桨。
②玉箫金管:用玉、金装饰的长箫和笛子。此处代指演奏乐器的歌妓。
③屈平:屈原。

这首诗以江上遨游起兴,表现了诗人对庸俗、局促的现实的鄙弃,对自由美好的生活理想的追求。开头四句夸饰的描写,展现了一个超世绝尘、自由美好的理想化世界。五、六句诗人自比海客,借黄鹤之典,表达忘机之心。七、八句将屈原、楚王的两种典型人生作了鲜明对比,语有警意。九、

Song on the River

In a ship of spice-wood with unsinkable oars,
Musicians at both ends, we drift along the shores.
We have sweet wine with singing girls to drink our fill,
And so the waves may carry us where'er they will.
Immortals could not fly without their yellow cranes;
Unselfish men might follow white gulls to the main.
The verse of Qu Ping shines as bright as sun and moon,
While palaces of Chu vanish like dreams at noon.
Seeing my pen in verve, even the mountains shake;
Hearing my laughter proud, the seaside hermits wake.
If worldly fame and wealth were things to last forever,
Then northwestward would turn the eastward-flowing river.

十两句活画出诗人摇笔赋诗时藐视一切、傲岸不羁的形象。最后两句表达了对淡泊清净的人格追求，对功名富贵的鄙薄。此诗为李白三四十岁时的大成之作，在思想上和艺术上，也很能代表李白诗歌特色，气势磅礴，气象恢弘，流转自如。

夜宿山寺

危①楼高百尺②,
手可摘星辰。
不敢高声语,
恐惊天上人。

① 危:高。
② 百尺:虚指,形容楼极高。

　　此五绝记游写景,通俗易懂。诗人夜宿寺庙。"危楼",呈现出山寺屹立山巅、高接天宇的非凡气势;"摘星辰""惊天人",也旨在表现山寺高耸的宏伟景象。用字如儿童天真的话语,字字平常,句句惊人,想象瑰丽,夸张巧妙,堪称"平字见奇"的绝世佳作。

The Summit Temple

Hundred feet high the Summit Temple stands,
Where I could pluck the stars with my own hands.
At dead of night I dare not speak aloud
For fear of waking dwellers in the cloud.

庐山谣寄卢侍御虚舟

我本楚狂人,
凤歌笑孔丘。
手持绿玉杖①,
朝别黄鹤楼。
五岳寻仙不辞远,
一生好入名山游。
庐山秀出南斗②傍,
屏风九叠云锦张,
影落明湖青黛③光。
金阙④前开二峰长,
银河⑤倒挂三石梁。
香炉瀑布遥相望,
回崖沓嶂凌苍苍。

①绿玉杖:镶嵌绿玉的手杖,传说中为仙人所用。
②南斗:星宿名,二十八宿之斗宿。
③青黛:青黑色。
④金阙:黄金的门楼,此处指庐山石门。
⑤银河:指瀑布。

唐肃宗上元元年(760),李白流放夜郎途中遇赦,从江夏往浔阳重游庐山。当时李白已经历尽磨难,始终不愿向折磨他的现实低头,求仙学道的心情更加迫切。此诗开头抒怀述志,继而写庐山风景,作结表达归隐求仙之愿望,不仅浓墨重彩地描绘了庐山秀丽雄奇的景色,更表现了诗人狂放不

Song of Mount Lu—To Censor Lu Xuzhou

I'm just a freak come from the South,

With frank advice e'er in my mouth.

Holding at dawn a green-jade cane,

I leave the Tower of Yellow Crane.

Of the long trips to Sacred Mountains I make light,

All my life I have loved to visit famous height.

Lu Mountains tower high beside the wain stars bright

Like a nine-panelled screen embroidered with clouds white.

Their shadows fall into the lake like emerald;

Two peaks stand face to face above the Gate of Gold.

A waterfall is hanging down from Three Stone Beams,

Cascades of Censer Peak like upended silver streams.

Cliff on cliff, ridge on ridge lead to the azure skies,

羁的性格,以及政治理想破灭后想要寄情山水、避世求仙的愤世之情。

翠影红霞映朝日,
鸟飞不到吴天长。
登高壮观天地间,
大江茫茫去不还。
黄云万里动风色,
白波九道流雪山。
好为庐山谣,
兴因庐山发。
闲窥石镜清我心,
谢公⑥行处苍苔没。
早服还丹无世情,
琴心三叠⑦道初成。
遥见仙人彩云里,
手把芙蓉朝玉京。
先期汗漫九垓⑧上,
愿接卢敖⑨游太清⑩。

⑥谢公:指谢灵运。
⑦琴心三叠:道家术语,指练功练到心和气静。
⑧九垓:九天之外。
⑨卢敖:战国时燕国人,对秦时的政治、军事、文化以及秦始皇的思想和行为都产生过影响。《淮南子》将他塑造成具备道家意味的寓言式人物,遂游六合,直至九天云外。
⑩太清:太空。

Their green shapes kindled by flaming clouds at sunrise
Barring the boundless Heaven's vault where no bird flies.
I climb to view the sky o'erhead and earth below,
The ne'er-returning waves of the River onward go.
In yellow clouds outspread for miles I see wind blow,
Nine foaming tributaries splash like mountain snow.
Of Mountain Lu I love to sing,
Of my poetry it is the spring.
I gaze at the Stone Mirror, my heart purified,
I seek the poet Xie's path which green mosses hide.
Elixir swallowed, I care not what people say;
The zither played thrice, I begin to know the Way.
I see from afar immortals in the cloudy land,
They come to celestial city, lotus-bloom in hand.
I'll go before you somewhere beyond the ninth sphere
And wait for you to wander in the Zenith Clear.

豫章行①

胡风②吹代马③,
北拥鲁阳关。
吴兵④照海雪,
西讨何时还?
半渡上辽津,
黄云惨无颜。
老母与子别,
呼天野草间。
白马绕旌旗,
悲鸣相追攀。
白杨秋月苦,
早落豫章山。

①豫章行:乐府旧题。
②胡风:北风。
③代马:代地(今山西省东北和河北省蔚县一带)所产的马匹。
④吴兵:吴越之地的士兵。

　　李白晚年目睹了安史之乱,对现实社会有了更真切、更冷静的认识。于是,他的作品便从对自己身世的忧愤转为对国事与民生的深深忧虑。唐肃宗上元元年(760),李白回到豫章(今江西南昌),亲眼目睹了新征士兵出征前妻儿老小呼天抢地的悲怆场面,百感交集,写下了这首诗。一方面对战

Song of Yuzhang

The horses neigh to hear the north wind blow,
The rebels occupy the Northern Pass.
The Southern armour bright as lake-side snow,
When will our men be back from war? Alas!
Half of them are aboard, ready to part,
E'en yellow clouds look gloomy and turn pale.
Old mothers see their sons off, sad at heart,
Crawling amid wild grass, they weep and wail.
Around the flags turn steeds which parting grieves,
They chase each other, foaming at the mouth.
'Neath autumn moon the poplars shed their leaves
Early which cover mountains of the South.

乱给百姓造成的苦难深表同情，另一方面又鼓励征人顾全大局，支持平叛战争。这与诗圣杜甫"三吏""三别"所表达的忧国忧民之情极其相似。《豫章行》古曲专写别离之苦，李白此诗却冲破了前人"皆伤离别"的狭小天地，赋予诗歌深刻的社会内容，不愧为现实主义杰作。

本为休明人,
斩虏素不闲⑤。
岂惜战斗死,
为君扫凶顽⑥。
精感石没羽,
岂云惮险艰?
楼船若鲸飞,
波荡落星湾。
此曲不可奏,
三军⑦发成斑。

⑤闲:同"娴",娴熟。
⑥凶顽:指凶残之人。
⑦三军:古代指步、车、骑三军。

I am a man living in time of peace,

Not used to fighting or exchanging blows.

But I am not afraid to fight without cease,

And sweep away our formidable foes.

Our concentrated efforts could break stone

And enemy however hard they are.

Our galleons swift like whales which might have flown

O'er waves which surge in the Bay of Falling Star.

This isn't a tune for army-men to play:

On hearing it, their hair would soon turn grey!

哭宣城善酿①纪叟

纪叟黄泉里，
还应酿老春②。
夜台③无李白，
沽④酒与何人？

①善酿：擅长酿酒。
②老春：纪叟所酿酒之名。
③夜台：坟墓。
④沽：卖。

纪叟，乃宣城一个善长酿酒的老头。现在他死了，李白大哭哀悼。一个普通平民，一个时代大诗人，因酒结缘。可怜的纪老头在阴间应会酿出甘美的老春酒，但那里没有李白，美酒又能卖给谁呢？言外之意，唯李白懂纪叟的酒，纪叟也专为诗人酿酒。现在阴阳相隔，知音难寻啊。生活琐屑大胆想象，真切悲伤尽聚笔端，表现出诗人纯朴友善的性格。

Elegy on Master Brewer Ji of Xuancheng

For thirsty souls are you still brewing

Good wine of Old Spring, Master Ji?

In underworld are you not ruing

To lose a connoisseur like me?

宣城见杜鹃花

蜀国曾闻子规鸟,
宣城还见杜鹃花①。
一叫一回肠一断,
三春三月忆三巴。

①杜鹃花：映山红。每年春末开放，恰是杜鹃鸟啼叫之时，故名杜鹃花。

二十四岁"仗剑去国，辞亲远游"，豪气干云闯天下，哪知飘蓬一世，求仙无成求仕无门，晚年抱老病残躯困居宣城——杜鹃朵朵开，杜鹃声声啼：不如归去！不如归去！如何归？归何处？一声一声愁肠断，寸寸乡思寸寸灰！苍茫无涯的愁思笼罩着诗人，字字泣出肺腑，凄苦令人不忍卒读。

Azalea Blooms Viewed in Xuancheng

I've heard home-going cuckoos sing in Western Towers ,
And here and now I see the blooming cuckoo flowers,
I turn away: my heart will break to hear them sing,
For they remind me of my homeland in late spring.

临终歌

大鹏飞兮振八裔①,
中天②摧兮力不济。
余风激兮万世,
游扶桑兮挂③左袂。
后人得之传此,
仲尼亡兮谁为出涕?

①八裔:八方边远地区。
②中天:半空。
③挂:比喻腐朽权势阻挠。

这首诗可看作李白自撰的墓志铭,系代宗宝应元年(762),李白病死于安徽当涂县前所作。李白既有远大的理想,又执着于理想,追求了一生。诗人将自己比作奋飞的大鹏,虽被摧折,余风仍可激扬万世。此诗让我们看到,他在对自己的一生进行回顾与总结的时候,流露的是对人生无比的眷念和未能才尽其用的深沉惋惜。

On Death-Bed

When flies the roc, he shakes the world.
In mid-air his weakened wings are furled.
The wind he's raised still stirs the sea,
He hangs his left wing on sun-side tree.
Posterity mine, hear, O, hear!
Confucius dead, who'll shed a tear?